Santa's
SECRET

Santa's SECRET

BY
CHRISTY HARDMAN
AND
PHIL PORTER

Bonneville Books
Springville, Utah

ISBN 13: 978-1-59955-178-4

Published by Bonneville, an imprint of Cedar Fort, Inc., 2373 W. 700 S., Springville, UT 84663
Distributed by Cedar Fort, Inc. www.cedarfort.com

LIBRARY OF CONGRESS CATALOGING-IN-PUBLICATION DATA

Hardman, Christy.
  Santa's secret / Christy Hardman and Phil Porter.
    p. cm.
  ISBN 978-1-59955-178-4 (alk. paper)
  I. Porter, Phil (Phillip Tanner), 1955- II. Title.

PS3608.A7254S26 2008
813'.6--dc22

                          2008014323

Cover design by Nicole Williams
Cover design © 2008 by Lyle Mortimer
Edited and typeset by Melissa J. Caldwell

Printed in the United States of America

10 9 8 7 6 5 4 3 2 1

Printed on acid-free paper

Other books by Christy Hardman

Against the Giant

Santa's Secret Wish

On Christmas Eve, a young boy with light in his eyes
Looked deep into Santa's, to Santa's surprise,

And said as he sat on Santa's broad knee,
"I want your secret. Tell it to me.

I want to know how, as you travel about,
Giving gifts here and there, you never run out.

How is it, dear Santa, that in your pack of toys
You have plenty for all of the world's girls and boys?

Your bag is all bulging, it fills up the sleigh
Stays full, never empties, as you make your way

From rooftop to rooftop, to homes large and small,
From nation to nation, reaching them all?"

And Santa smiled kindly and said to the boy,
"Don't ask me hard questions. Don't you want a toy?"

But the child shook his head, and Santa could see
That he needed the answer. "Now listen to me,"

He told that small boy with the light in his eyes,
"My secret will make you sadder and wise.

The truth is that my sack is magic. Inside
It holds millions of toys for my Christmas Eve ride.

But although I do visit each girl and boy
I don't always leave them a gaily wrapped toy.

Some homes are hungry, some homes are sad,
Some homes are desperate, some homes are bad.

Some homes are broken, and the children there grieve.
Those homes I visit, but what should I leave?

My sleigh is filled with the happiest stuff,
But for the homes where despair lives, toys aren't enough.

So I tiptoe in, kiss each girl and boy,
And I pray with them that they'll be given the joy

Of the Spirit of Christmas, the Spirit that lives
In the heart of the dear child who gets not, but gives.

If only God hears me and answers my prayer,
When I visit next year, what I will find there

Are homes filled with peace, and with giving and love
And boys and girls gifted with light from above.

It's a very hard task, my smart little brother,
To give toys to some, and to give prayers to others.

But the prayers are the best gifts, the best gifts indeed,
For God has a way of meeting each need.

That's part of the answer. The rest, my dear youth,
Is that my sack is magic. And that is the truth.

In my sack I carry on Christmas Eve day
More love than a Santa could e'er give away.

The sack never empties of love, or of joys
'Cause inside it are prayers, and hope, not just toys.

The more that I give, the fuller it seems,
Because giving is my way of fulfilling dreams.

And do you know something? You've got a sack too.
It's as magic as mine, and it's inside of you.

It never gets empty, it's full from the start
It's the center of lights and love. It's your heart.

And if on this Christmas you want to help me,
Don't be so concerned with the gifts 'neath your tree.

Open that sack called your heart, and share
Your joy, your friendship, your wealth, your care."

The light in the small boy's eyes was glowing.
"Thanks for your secret. I've got to be going."

"Wait, little boy," said Santa, "don't go.
Will you share? Will you help? Will you use what you know?"

And just for a moment the small boy stood still,
Touched his heart with his small hand, and whispered, "I will."

—Betty Worth Westrope

1

Phil opened the box and breathed in the faint mustiness of age and seasoned cardboard. He pulled out the plastic garbage bag, tore it open, and ran his fingers through the curls of the white wig and beard. He picked them up and placed them down gently onto the spare room bed. The fur of the red suit was soft and familiar. Phil flapped the suit out into the air. The fur always had a strange distinctive smell, even after he'd had it dry cleaned. After a year of sitting in the box, the suit smelled stronger. It was the smell of Christmas.

You could tell a lot about a person from the clothes he wore. You could tell what he did for a living, at least come fairly close. You could tell whether he was well to do or down on his luck. You could tell if he was meticulous about ironing and grooming. There was something recognizable in anyone's outfit that categorized them. Which was why he loved putting this suit on. When he put on the costume, he was the most recognizable man in the world.

Phil laid them all out on the bed—the hat, wig, beard, suit, padding, and boots. He took down the box that had his Santa Claus watch, and last of all, the oblong case that held his glasses.

He couldn't help the happy grin that spread across his face. Beneath the faint smell of dust he'd disturbed, he could smell the turkey Mom had just taken from the oven, and with it the soft clank of the plates against the table. The buzzer on the oven went off, and Aunt Cathy would be pulling her prize-winning yams from the oven, and the rolls would be steaming beside the honey butter on the table. From the window came the voices of the kids and Phil's older sons, all of them screaming as somebody scored a touchdown on the front lawn. Thanksgiving Day always marked the beginning of it, his favorite time of year: the Christmas season, when he dressed up in this suit and became Santa Claus. In his opinion, it was the only way to experience Christmas. After all these years—he closed his eyes, counting back—yes, it was twenty-seven years now—he didn't know any other way.

Maybe he'd just quickly try the suit on before dinner. What would it hurt? He had to see how much padding he'd need before the parade tomorrow night anyway.

He picked up the pants and started working his foot into them when he stopped.

"Oh, yeah," he groaned, inspecting the seam in the crotch. The fabric was worn, and the seam was tearing out altogether. He'd forgotten when he put it away last year that this suit was almost in its death throes. He puffed out his cheeks and blew the air out heavily. Maybe he could convince Denise, his wife, to make him another suit . . . but before Christmas? He shook his head. There was no way he'd convince her to take on that mess. And where would she sew it? Not at their house with Andrew running through with his fourth grader friends all the day long.

Phil rummaged through the top drawer of the dresser and came back with a roll of duct tape.

"Ah-ha!" There wasn't much that couldn't be fixed with a little ingenuity and a roll of duct tape. The tape screeched as he pulled off a long piece, and then fitting it from the inside out, taped the seam back together so it wouldn't show. Not a bad job all in all.

The doorknob rattled, and Phil jumped, hopping in front of the suit, but he needn't have bothered. He'd locked the door. Made sure of that.

"Dad! Dad, are you in there?"

"Yep, I'm here, Andy. Just . . . tidying up. I'll be right out."

"Grandma Phyllis wants you to carve the turkey now. She says to come."

"All right." Phil stuffed the suit back into the closet, draping the shoulders across a hanger, and dusted his hands off. "Tell her I'll be right there." He almost reached for the doorknob when he turned and snatched the wig and beard off the bed and plopped them on top of the mannequin head. He shoved it back as far as it would go on the top shelf of the closet and then tucked the watch, glasses, and bag of padding after it.

Five minutes later Phil was carving up the bird, snatching a bite here and there of hot turkey right off the bones. Man, he loved this time of year.

"What is it you're humming there?" Phyllis asked him, and Phil looked up, blinking. He didn't realize he was humming.

"Oh, it's 'Here Comes Santa Claus,' " Denise said from where she was setting out napkins on the table. "He must have snuck off and took a peek at his suit. I swear it's nothing short of a love affair."

"Well, it could be worse," Phyllis said, chuckling, "than a man obsessed with playing Santa Claus."

"Shh," Phil told them both, jerking his head toward the living room where his youngest son, Andrew, was glued to the screen, his thumb popping out bullets into the enemy ships.

"He's not listening," Denise said.

"Phil, you know you're going to have to tell him this year. For heaven's sake, he's nine years old! He's getting past the age of believing anyway."

"You'll never convince him to tell, Phyllis," Denise said, setting the gravy boat down on the tablecloth. "To him, believing in Santa Claus is next to going to church. It's a religion, and I'm not kidding."

Phil tucked a slice of white meat beside the stack of dark. "Isn't that what Christmas is all about, though? Believing in something bigger and better than what you have in the here and now? It's about making the Christmas magic real; you know, that kind of magic you could only have when you were a kid. That's the appeal for me, I guess. When I'm in that suit, I am the magic of Christmas, and I can give that away to everyone I see."

"Yes, you and your magic," Phyllis said. She grunted under the load of mashed potatoes and set the huge serving dish down on the table with a loud thunk. "All I can say is that I want all that junk out of my spare room. It's time you started changing at your own house. Magic me that."

Phil put the tray of turkey down in the center of the table, and raising his hands to his mouth, blew out a trumpet sound.

"Come and eat!" he called, and Mom's words were drowned out by the stampede that followed as everybody swarmed in around the table.

2

Phil had seen a lot of children the Saturday after Thanksgiving. It had been an especially busy day, actually. Now while there was a bit of a lull, he just sat and watched them—watched their parents too. You could tell a lot of things that way, whether the kids were really good like they said, and how the parents treated their children. You could see it in the kids' faces, in their eyes.

He'd heard a lot of Christmas wishes from the children already. Let's see. He had over ten requests for that new powered up truck thing Tonka had just put out, and no less than fifteen girls wanted that pink pony castle. One kid even asked for a snow blower. Go figure.

After all these years, he still never got tired of the way the kids' eyes shone when they saw his white beard and bright red suit, the way they laughed when they heard his bells. There was nothing like the pure, straight joy bubbling out of young kids. It came out of every part of them. Even their feet would start up dancing, like they heard a kind of music in the jingling.

But the boy that was looking at him now was not smiling. He ducked his head back around the corner. Santa Claus kept watching, giving him a smile for encouragement. He waited. The boy would come back. And he did, first the tips of his sticking-out blond hair, then his round forehead, and finally his eyes peeked back around. They were big blue eyes. Cute kid.

"Come on," Santa said, gesturing with his hand toward the

boy. "Come here, buddy. Come and see me."

The head disappeared again, but Santa waited. It was not too unusual that a child was afraid of him. He had seen this kind of thing before, when kids were afraid. It started when they were two. Every two-year-old was afraid of Santa Claus. Of course they were. Here comes this huge man dressed in a bright red suit with a big old beard covering his whole face—not to mention the noise, what with the bells and ho-ho-ho-ing. An all around scary experience if it wasn't handled right. The trick was to not force the kid before he was ready. So Santa waited. There was time. The aisles were strangely empty. The boy would come around.

"Come on, buddy," he said again when the boy's head appeared back around the corner. The boy's eyes looked one way, then the other, like he was afraid to be seen. Santa saw him suck in a big breath, but there he went again, back behind the aisle. Santa hummed through a song, got all the way to "Oh by golly, have a holly jolly Christmas" before the boy peeked out again. This time he came, started coming up the aisle toward him.

Santa held himself still, didn't react outwardly, but he couldn't help his eyes blinking fast behind his glasses. Unbelievable!

The boy was wearing a cream-colored adult coat—well, once it had been cream-colored. It was hard to tell through the grime. The zipper was broken, and it hung limp and crooked on his little body. His T-shirt beneath the coat was ragged, showing bare skin in a couple of places. The pants could have fit around Santa's own big bulk.

Santa leaned forward, scrunching up his eyes. The pants were held on by a frayed rope threaded through the belt loops. The boy's feet were coming through huge holes in the knees of the pants, and the legs of the pants were pulling along behind him, dragging against the floor as he walked. His bare feet were poking through the toes of his shoes that were so big, Santa couldn't figure how they even stayed on.

The boy shuffled toward Santa and stopped, didn't even raise his head from staring at the floor.

There were a lot of things Santa Claus could do now. He could wait until the boy was brave enough to speak, maybe give him a minute to not feel so shy. But sometimes there was a kid that just cried out for love just by standing there. At that point, there was nothing else to be done. Santa scooped him right up onto his knee. He hugged his thin body, and he didn't mind the smell of dirt and sweat and heaven only knew what else.

"Hey, buddy," Santa said, smiling down into his face. He gave the boy a squeeze. "Merry Christmas. What's your name?"

The boy swiped a hand under his runny nose.

"Cody."

"Well, Cody. Tell me, what do you want for Christmas?"

He looked up at him with big blue eyes and studied Santa for a minute—a serious study, with lips pressed out. Then he said, "Santa Claus, I want a bed."

"You want a what?" Even after all these years, the children still caught him off guard.

"I want a bed," he said, meeting Santa's eyes. The boy swallowed, his neck showing streaks of dirt and grime. "Because we have a pretty big family, and I'm the youngest, and all my brothers and sisters and my parents have beds to sleep on. But I sleep on the rag pile in the corner."

For a minute Santa couldn't speak at all. He pressed his lips together, blinking to keep the tears from showing. He reached up and patted the kid's head. The hair was matted and dirty.

"A bed," Santa repeated. A bed! In all his days, he'd never heard anything like it. Mostly he just nodded to kids' requests for Christmas things, gave the mom or dad a grin and a wink. Sometimes the kids would get what they asked for, sometimes not. Mostly it didn't matter too much. The magic was in the experience—the kids being able to sit on Santa's lap, to have that moment of Christmas that was pure childhood magic. But this time there wouldn't be that kind of nod.

Santa looked straight at him and said, "Okay, Cody, I'll see what I can do."

The boy smiled. "Thank you, Santa Claus."

Santa reached into his bag and held out a candy cane. Cody's dirty fingers closed around it.

"Thanks!" The smile lit Cody's face. His eyes literally glowed. He was still smiling when he hopped off Santa's lap and ran off.

Santa watched him, those ridiculous pant legs dragging on behind him. He was heading for the door. Santa looked around quick. There was no one in sight. He got off his chair, started to follow the kid—but it couldn't be him to follow Cody. He looked around again. The kid was almost out the door.

A store clerk came up the aisle just then, and Santa practically pounced on him.

"Come here!" Santa motioned. "Hurry! Come here."

The clerk stopped, jerked his head over his shoulder. "What?"

"I need you to do something for me."

"Hey man, I'm busy," the clerk said, already walking away. "I've got to . . ."

"No, don't . . . Look, I need you to do something for me, and it's got to be quick." He kept talking, right over the top of the clerk's excuses. "You see that little guy that just run off? See, he just left the store. Would you do something for me?"

"Hey, I'm busy . . ."

Santa kept on. "Please, please. You have to tell me . . . I've got to find out who that little boy is. He asked for something special, and I need his name, his address, and his parents' names and their telephone number. Please! I have to have it."

The clerk tried to pull away, but Santa wouldn't look away. He let there be silence between them. It was another thing he found out a long time ago. It was hard for people to say no to Santa Claus.

The clerk's eyes rolled up while he let out his breath, and Santa smiled and knew he had him.

"Oh, all right, I'll do it."

Santa gave his arm a hard pat. "Thank you." But the clerk was already heading in a half-jog after the boy.

Santa watched him go, putting a curled hand to his mouth.

"Hurry," he whispered behind his hand. He sat back down on his chair.

He slept on the rag pile in the corner.

Unbelievable.

Another kid ran up and climbed on his lap, voiced his request, and ran off in less than a minute. Santa turned his hand, palm side up, and glanced at his watch. The gold second hand ticked around the Santa Claus face while overhead a woman's voice interrupted Bing Crosby's "White Christmas" to announce the day's special sales. What would he do if the clerk didn't find the boy? Cody hadn't even given his last name. There was no way he could . . .

Then there he was. The clerk jogged back through the swishing front door, and Santa's face split into a smile.

"There you go," the clerk said, and he was smiling now too. Christmas did that to people. The clerk put the slip of paper into Santa's hand. Santa glanced at it, saw the scrawled names and numbers that belonged to Cody, giving him a home, an identity, beyond a first name.

"Thank you!" Santa said, clutching the paper. "Thank you."

"You bet," the clerk said, still smiling. It had happened to him, Santa could tell. The clerk had felt the magic just in talking to the kid, had felt the joy of being part of the giving. "Any time," the clerk said as he walked away. "You just let me know."

Santa lifted a hand in a half wave, half salute, and the clerk was gone. Santa read over the address again, and then folded the slip of paper and put it into his pocket.

Phil told Denise about it before he went to bed, which was probably why he was still thinking about it, laying awake, here in his own comfortable bed. How in the world would he get a bed for that little guy? Maybe he could . . . no, it was too close to Christmas. Only three and a half weeks away.

"Denise?"

"Hmm?"

"I was just thinking . . ."

She shifted but didn't turn over to face him.

"What if we asked Hank Johnson. He's always got extra wood, and maybe we could . . .?"

"What are you talking about? Is this about that little boy and his bed again?"

Phil scrunched down a little under the covers. "Well. Yeah. I just think if we—"

"Honey, it's almost twelve thirty. There's church in the morning. Can't we talk about it more tomorrow?"

Phil reached a hand across his head to scratch at his opposite ear. "I just . . . I can't get his face out of my head."

"Go to sleep, Phil."

He sighed. "Yeah."

He rubbed a hand over his mouth and chin, scratching at the blond stubble that would come off tomorrow. It always itched under his Santa Claus beard. Then he looked up at the ceiling, slipped out from under the covers, and went on to his knees.

"Father in Heaven," he whispered low so as to not disturb Denise, "I told him I'd get him a bed. You know I don't have time—and money's tight this year what with the new transmission on the truck. But I promised. I told him I would. Please help me know what to do."

He climbed back into bed, and another face came into his head, another boy who had come in that same day, just a few hours after Cody had gone.

He had come in with his mother, dressed head to foot in San Francisco 49ers duds, even had 49ers stocking cap. Probably had 49ers underoos too. His dad must be a real fan.

"Come on," the kid's mom said, practically dragging the kid. "Come and see Santa Claus."

"I don't want to see Santa. He's dumb."

Santa forced a smile, but his eyes narrowed just a bit behind his glasses.

"Just come on." She pulled on the kid's hand, dragging him forward. The boy stopped right in front of Santa, rolling the immaculate toe of his 49ers shoe on the tile floor. His face was set in a pout.

"Tell him what you want for Christmas," his mom said.

The boy gave a half shrug and rolled his eyes, but he climbed up on Santa's knee, balancing there. Santa let him hold himself up, hardly touched him with his hand behind his back.

"Well, then," another forced smile, "tell me what's your name?"

"Name's Alan Brodrick Grady." There was no other word for him but *sullen*.

"Well, Alan, what—"

"Alan Brodrick Grady. I told you it's Alan Brodrick Grady. You must be the stupidest Santa I've ever seen."

Santa's face heated beneath his beard. If only he could turn the kid over his knee and give him what he deserved for Christmas. Santa took a slow, calming breath.

"Okay, Alan Brodrick Grady. Tell me what you want for Christmas."

"You know that new Power Truck thing that roars up and down hills and all? I want one of those. Plus, I want a Playstation 3, and all the games. Plus a Wii. And all the games. And I want a dune buggy. One like I saw in the mall. It had these really cool black shiny running boards, not the dumb one without the running boards like you sell here, and you better get it right." Alan Brodrick Grady rolled his eyes at his mom, who was moving her head like a bobblehead doll, nodding her head at everything he said.

"Oh, and Santa," Alan Brodrick Grady said, squinting up at him, "you better bring it all, or I'll be mad at you."

He pushed off Santa's chest, stomping both his feet down onto the ground. He snatched a candy cane right out of Santa's bag and dashed off, shooting spit noises with his hands.

"Alan Brodrick!" Mom called after him, but he kicked at a ball in the ball tube, sending the balls scattering and bouncing all over the floor, and dashed around the corner.

Santa looked at Mom while his mind did some quick figures. Andrew was close to Alan Brodrick Grady's age. He'd like some of those things too. But he sure knew better than to ask for them.

"You're not really going to get him all of that, are you?" Santa asked Mom.

"Of course," she said, hardly giving him a look. "My husband and I feel very strongly that we should go all out for Christmas."

The balls were rolling all over, and Grady's mom wasn't making a move to clean them up. "He must be an only child then," Santa said.

"Oh no. He has an older sister. Christmas is a special holiday." She gave him a level look. "You of all people should know that."

"Oh. Oh, well, good luck. You have a merry Christmas." He had given her a wave as she strolled off after her spoiled kid.

Phil sat up in bed, the two faces of those little boys spinning around in his head. He leaned over Denise, who was snoring soundly. Just to be sure, he gave her a little poke. She didn't stir. He turned on his bedside lamp and shuffled in the side table drawer. At last he found a piece of paper and scratched a note to himself.

"Find a bed for Cody." He underlined it three times, and then he crawled back into bed. A few minutes later he turned the light back on and added another item to the list.

"Get a new Santa Claus suit."

The next night Phil had two appointments. He gave the business party a final wave. They cheered and clapped as he jingled himself out the door.

He had a little less than half an hour to get to his next party. It was a family party he had visited every Christmas for twenty-some-odd years. It was just the right night for it. He was already stoked and excited from his success with Tyrell Inc., and the Christensen family was always one of his favorites. Their energy and excitement was contagious.

The air was crisp and clear, his breath coming out in mists of white frost against the darkness. His fur-topped Santa boots crunched in the snow, black against white, and the jingle of his bells sounded clean and sharp in the cold. Christmas lights twinkled from the houses, glowing off the snow, and the windows shone out rectangles of light where families were inside, eating dinner or sharing a laugh. Lights blinked on the houses, red, white, green, and blue. All of this together was Christmas, and he was part of it in his red suit and white beard. He stepped lighter, kicking up a clump of snow.

"Dashing through the snow in a one horse open sleigh . . . !" Phil sang as he packed his big bag into the seat beside him in his truck.

He passed a minivan stuffed full of kids who waved and pointed, shouting and smiling behind their car windows. He honked and waved. Their faces pressed against the back window as he drove past. Phil chuckled.

"Oh, what fun it is to ride in a one horse open sleigh!"

The Christensen house was at the end of the street, packed with cars. He'd been here so many times it was almost like coming home. Smiling, he pulled his truck alongside the curb and put the brake on. He glanced at his wrist, palm side up. Seven twenty-six. Perfect. He got out, shouldered his bag, and started crunching up the hill through the snow.

At the front door he paused, anticipating the shouts and squeals that would greet him the minute he opened it. He stood perfectly still so his bells wouldn't give him away. Then three quick knocks, and he pushed the door open a crack. The room was packed, people stuffed into every single corner. He smiled. No one had noticed him yet. Then quietly, so quietly, he jingled his bells.

Several of the kids jumped up and started shouting. He jingled again, and while the kids broke into grins and started popping up like popcorn, he came in.

"Merry Christmas! Ho ho ho!"

"It's Santa! It's Santa!"

"Ho ho ho!"

It was mostly the littlest kids dashing around, yelling, but the older ones, the kids between six and eleven, were sitting still. Some of them weren't even smiling. John, maybe ten-ish now, even looked away when Santa smiled at him. Santa reached out and patted the head of a little boy dashing around his legs.

"Now, sit down all of you," Grandma Lorraine said. "We'll put Santa Claus over here. Come on, right here." She led him to the armchair in the corner, and the little kids gathered at his feet, all of them pushing and shoving to get closer. Some of the kids scooted in, but others hung back, and some looked toward their mom or dad as if to ask permission. Lorraine's eyes looked puffy and red, and she wiped a hand at her cheek. The adults were talking in hushed tones in little clumps here and there around the room. No one was laughing or even smiling.

Last year when he'd come, he was bombarded at the door, almost knocked right off his feet. The kids pulled him into the house, and the adults gathered around, as eager to participate as the kids. They were always laughing and joking, setting each other off. And so much noise!

But this year . . .

The sound of his movement, his tinkling bells, the crackle of the wrapped presents inside his bag, all sounded so loud in the hush that hung over them.

He made his way through the names of the presents in his bags, pulling the kids onto his lap one by one, but he had to lean his ear in close to the kids' mouths. Even the smallest ones wouldn't do more than whisper. Most of the girls were in dresses, and the boys were in ties and slacks, and they just sat there like they were in Sunday School.

"There's a good boy," he said to little Joel, who hopped off his lap and tore into his present. "Well, then." Santa looked into his bag. Empty. "Is that everyone then?"

No one really answered him. No one was really looking at him. Except Lorraine. She kept darting glances in his direction and biting her lip. This had to be the strangest party he'd ever done.

"Well, then, I'll just . . . "

He was halfway up when the impression hit him.

"Did I miss anyone? Is there . . . is there anyone else who needs to come and talk to Santa Claus?"

What was he doing? He never ended his parties like this. He almost got up to cover for himself, but there it was again. He settled back in, lifted his head, and looked around.

The room got very still. Little Joel even stopped popping his sister in the head with his new dart gun and looked up at Santa, his eyes wide. There was a shuffling in the back of the room. One of the four-year-olds buried her head in her mama's neck and whimpered.

A man stood up in the back, a big tall guy and skinny, just skinny. He had on a ten-gallon-plus cowboy hat. There were gasps somewhere to Santa's right, and the kids at Santa's feet scooted back. Little Hannah ran back to her mom with her arms outstretched.

Lorraine covered her mouth with her hands. Santa saw all of this, but his eyes were fixed on the man coming toward him, the people parting for him this way and that like the Red Sea. He came to stand in front of Santa, who looked straight up into his face. He was a young guy, early twenties maybe. He bent his lanky form and sat down on Santa's lap. Santa cleared his throat. The man wasn't smiling. All eyes were stuck right onto them. Santa rubbed his beard.

"Well, now. What's your name?"

"Name's Mick."

The man wasn't making this any easier.

"Well, Mick. Are you being good?"

Mick was looking right into his face.

"Nope. I'm not being good at all, Santa Claus. But I'm trying." His breath caught, and came out a little shaky. "I'm going to try to be a better person."

"Well. All right." Santa cleared his throat again. "All right, then. What do you want for Christmas?"

Mick pressed his mouth closed, and the muscles in his neck worked beneath his collar. He wasn't looking at Santa any more.

"I . . . I can't talk about that right now."

One of the men standing to their right folded his arms, leaned clear back into the wall, and one of the women dabbed at her eyes.

Well, what now? Santa stroked his beard again.

"Okay. You say you haven't been good, and you can't talk about what you want for Christmas. So what are we doing here?" Santa asked.

The man drew in a breath and let it out again. He took off

his cowboy hat, showing a head of pressed-down blond hair. He rubbed a hand through his hair, and then put his hat back on.

"Well, I guess I'm sitting here in proxy for my three-year-old daughter. We buried her today."

Santa barely caught the gasp in his throat. He shot a look at Lorraine. What in the world was she doing having a family Christmas party on the same day she buried her granddaughter? What was she thinking?

Santa's face felt hot. He wanted to take off his hat, wig, and all, and rub his own head. But the kids were watching. They needed something now. Mick needed something.

"Oh. Oh, well, I want to thank you for telling me," Santa said. "I'm sure your daughter was on the nice list, and sometimes when the children are on the nice list, we don't look in on them as often as we should because generally they don't change their ways this time of year. Because she's on the good list, you may have gotten some toys on Christmas Day that might not have been appreciated."

Inside his head, he was pleading desperately.

Help me. Help me to say something that will mean something to this man. Heavenly Father, please help me 'cause I've got to say something.

"But you know what?" Santa leaned toward Mick, making him meet his eyes. "They're going to have Christmas where she's at this year. They're going to have Christmas, and it's going to be a happy and fun time. And you know what else? She's going to be given some gifts. And the person who will give her those gifts is the same person whose birth we are celebrating at this time of year."

Tears that were gathering in Mick's eyes suddenly spilled over, and he brushed them off his cheeks.

"And those gifts will never be the wrong color," Santa said. "They will never wear out, and they will always be just right, because the gifts that He gives are gifts that last forever. They're eternal gifts."

Mick's body was shaking a little, and his mouth was fighting a frown that would break him clear down.

Santa kept talking.

"And when you become a better person, like you promised me you would, you can go visit her—when it's your turn to go there. When it's your turn." Santa brought up a finger. "Now's not the time to go there, but one day you'll be with her forever. But you have to do your part first."

There were sniffs from all sides of the room. More people were wiping at their eyes now. Mick turned right there on Santa's knee and wrapped his long arms all the way around him. Santa hugged him back, rocking him like a small child. Mick sniffed into his suit, and Santa patted his back. Finally Mick pulled back and stood up. Santa stood up beside him.

"You see here, kids," Mick said, waving a hand at the kids that were still clustered at their feet. "Grandma sure found us the real Santa Claus, because only the real Santa Claus could know what to say to make us feel a lot better."

Santa wiped at his own eyes, and Mick wrapped him up in a hug again, slapping him hard on the back. Then Santa leaned down, picked up his bag, handed Mick a candy cane, and went out the door.

He closed the door behind him. The night was silent, and the stars winked at him from their heights.

"Thank you," Santa said into the sky, and he lifted his hand in a salute to heaven. He started toward his truck, and was just reaching the edge of the driveway, when there was a call from the porch.

"Phil!"

He turned. Lorraine ran down the stairs, hurrying toward him.

"Phil!" She talked as she came closer, her shoes slapping against the concrete drive. "You know, I knew you were good, but I didn't know what was going to happen when he came up there. I wanted to warn you but I didn't know how. Where in the world did you come up with that?"

He waited until she was standing in front of him, and then he took a deep breath. "Well, sometimes the giver of gifts is given one, and you have just seen one of the best gifts that I have ever, ever received."

She nodded and sniffed. "It's been hard for us. Thank you," Lorraine said.

"It wasn't me." He swung up into his truck.

"Well, thank you, Santa Claus," she said. He waved and didn't correct her, even though that wasn't what he'd meant.

3

Christmas music piped over the overhead speakers. People were packed, completely packed, into the decorated aisles. And just like always, the kids were hanging off the grocery baskets and driving their parents nuts. The smell of gingerbread wafted over from the direction of the bakery where they had just set up their award-winning gingerbread village. Once in a while—it was a pity how rarely it really happened—someone came through with a smile and a merry Christmas to everyone they saw. Even the stockers and baggers at the store were usually too busy to really look around and enjoy what was happening, everybody rushing around to prepare something special for their loved ones. All of these people were living in a moment they would never remember because they were too busy to slow down and make it a memory.

As Santa Claus, Phil got a different perspective on holiday shopping, even here at the grocery store. These sorts of moments were the very essence of Christmas, this brush with humanity while he sat there in the middle of it all, a public figure. No one realized just how much their faces revealed as they walked through the grocery store or how much the contents of their grocery carts told about how they planned to spend their holiday.

He waved to little Yolanda as she stripped the paper from her candy cane and started in on it. She took her momma's hand and skipped off, content in her little world, having delivered her Christmas wish to the right ears.

Christmas was a simple thing to a child. It was tangible evidence of the workings of faith and prayer. The child hopped up onto Santa's lap, made herself known, and told it straight out what she wanted. A child could understand this sort of relationship, that she as an individual was known to a being who was far and away bigger than their own little sphere—and that their level of obedience and goodness mattered on that great of a scale. A child was certain in the knowledge that she would be rewarded for it.

While the child was up on his lap, delivering his Christmas wish, Santa knew he could trust Mom or Dad to take care of it, in the way they felt best, same as God had to leave many things to people here to answer the needs of His children. That was just one of the ways he had come closer to God by being Santa Claus.

Santa blinked. A little girl stood right in front of him, and he hadn't heard a sound of her coming.

"Well!" he said, and smiled. "Merry Christmas!" He held out his arms, but she hung back. Her eyes flashed to one side and then the other; then she darted a look into Santa's face. He gave her another smile and kept his hand outstretched.

"It's okay," he said quietly. "You come when you're ready. I'll wait right here." He gave her a smile, a little wave, and then put his hands on his knees and whistled "We Wish You a Merry Christmas." The words played over and over in his mind while the tune came out in his whistle. He looked up at the ceiling, and sure enough, by the end of the first chorus, he felt a small warm hand on his arm.

"Well." He smiled into the little girl's face. "Here you are."

She gave him a small smile.

"Do you want to sit up here on my lap?"

She nodded, her face solemn. She was a thin girl, and her hair hung straight on both sides of her narrow face. Her head was bowed, but her eyes watched him every second.

He held out his hands to her again, and this time she clambered up onto his lap.

"There you go," he said, giving her a squeeze. She held herself stiff, didn't give anything back.

"What's your name, sweetheart?" he asked.

" 'Lizabeth." Almost a whisper.

"Elizabeth. That's a beautiful name. Tell, me, Elizabeth, what is it you want for Christmas?"

She ducked her head and buried her words in the collar of her shirt. He leaned toward her, and she ducked her head even farther, curling up on herself. He tightened his hugging arm around her.

"What was that?"

She licked her lips. "I want my momma not to hit me any more."

"You want your momma not to hit you?" he whispered back.

She glanced up at him and back down again. She nodded.

Santa put his other hand to his beard, then put it back around her. He bent low to her face. This was only to be between them.

"Does your momma hit you a lot?"

Another nod.

"Does she hit you hard?"

The girl swallowed.

"Sometimes." A glance at his face. "Mostly."

He tightened his hug, closed his eyes.

Father, let her feel safe for this one moment.

Santa swallowed, and the song overhead finished with a flurry of jingle bells and trumpets. The shoppers rushed on all around them, and the speakers popped as someone called for cleanup on aisle nine. Her thin fingers played with the fur on the trim of his coat.

He took in a small breath and let it back out.

"Sweetheart, I don't know what to tell you. Sometimes words aren't enough to fix . . ."

Santa put a hand to his temple.

"But sometimes words can help. Maybe . . . maybe after your mom gets done with her hitting—and don't be smart aleck when you do this, but just be sweet and really as nice as you can be— maybe after you've quit crying, after the real physical hurt has eased up, maybe you can go up and tell your mother, 'Momma, I still love you, even if you do hit me.' "

She was watching him now, studying his face, and a little crease puckered between her eyes.

"Do you love your mother?" Santa asked her.

She nodded. "Oh yes. I love her really, really much."

"Then tell her."

She brushed the hair out of her face. "Hmm. I never thought of trying that." As she looked at him, her face changed and it was smiling, and her eyes were crinkled at the corners, and she had a darling dimple in her cheek.

Santa held out a candy cane, and she took it.

"Thank you, Santa Claus. I'll try it."

She hopped off his lap and walked away, but turned around and waved at him after five steps. And she was still smiling.

Santa saw them come in, and he broke into a grin. Of all people to see here. Mark Crawford. He hadn't seen him for over twenty years.

He had some pretty cute little kids too.

"Santa Claus!" they yelled, and started toward him.

Santa smiled and pulled the little boy up on his lap. Mark hung back, smiling at them with that I'm-glad-you're-my-kid-but-don't-embarrass-me smile that parents would sometimes get.

"Now what's your name?" Santa asked.

"I'm Sam, and this is my sister Jasmine."

"Well, Sam and Jasmine, have you been good this year?"

"Yep." Sam was matter of fact.

"And I believe you," Santa told him. "I even believe that your dad is good, now that he's big. But let me tell you, when he was a little boy, your dad . . . why one year he was so bad I couldn't even bring him a lump of coal."

Mark reared his head back, staring at Santa down his nose.

The kids looked from Santa to Dad, their faces split with matching grins.

Santa nodded at them, gave Mark a broad wink, and then gathered Jasmine up on his other knee.

"One summer, see, your dad went and stole one of his dad's

cigarette lighters. He and a couple of his buddies had decided to form a club. They took that old lighter and caught them some grasshoppers. They'd put that old grasshopper on a pin or a nail and roast it up, and anybody who wanted to join the club had to eat one of those grasshoppers."

"Dad! You did that?"

"He sure did," Santa said and chuckled. Mark's eyes were narrowed, studying Santa's face. "Of course, him and his little buddies that did this, why they never ate a grasshopper, no sir! Just told everybody that come along, 'Yeah, we did! Yeah, we did!'"

"Who the heck are you?" Mark asked, and Santa laughed and winked at Sam and Jasmine.

"Well, who do you think? I'm Santa Claus. I know everything."

"Dad, did you really do that?" Jasmine asked.

"Did the grasshoppers stink when you roasted them?" Sam asked.

Mark was still squinting into Santa Claus's face. "How did you know that? I can't quite figure out . . . Who are you anyway?"

Santa just smiled.

"Well, and here you are, Santa Claus." Judith McArthur, all four feet nine and a half inches of her, stood smiling at him beside her grocery cart.

"Judith! How are you?"

"I'm doing well, thank you." She touched her hair that was now completely silver. It had been nearly ten years since they'd worked together on the Christmas Chamber of Commerce project. While her hair was grayer, her face wasn't a day older, and the same old smile came beaming out at him.

"How's the Christmas shopping going?" he asked, glancing at her basket that was brimming full.

"Oh, well enough. Look at this. Can you believe it?" She thrust a package of yellow and orange striped candy canes at him, and he read the label.

"Piña colada?"

"Exactly. On a candy cane."

"Unbelievable. What they won't think of next." He handed the box back to her.

"Anyway, I just picked them up off the shelf so I could exclaim over it. I'm not really going to buy them, you know. I'm a traditional girl, myself," Judith told him, patting at her hair again. "Peppermint is the only flavor that should be in a candy cane in my book."

"I'm actually partial to cherry," Phil said, taking a candy cane from his bag and handing it to her. "Try it, and you'll see why."

"I will." She smiled that bright smile at him again. "And I'll share it with my grandbabies. I've got the twins tonight since Martha and Jasper are in town. They're off to the play, so I get the babies. I've got to cram all the happy memories I can into those kids while I have them." She sighed. "They just grow up way too fast, don't they?"

"Yeah," Phil said, thinking of his dilemma with Andrew. "What we all wouldn't give to hold them in their innocence a little while longer."

"Do you think they get it? Any of it anymore? It's such a different world than we knew when we were kids. So fast paced, so jam-packed with flashing lights and blaring sounds. Will our grandchildren ever get to know Jesus and the true meaning of Christmas when it has to compete with all of that?"

Phil shook his head. "It's a life's work," he said.

"What we need, what we really need, is more giving, more loving. Those kind of simple, real things, you know." She let out a sad sort of sigh. "Even with the babies visiting, I feel like Christmas is missing something. I would love to take on some project, something that will help me feel the true meaning of Christmas through all the hustle and bustle."

"Do you mean it?" Phil asked, the idea spinning in his head.

Judith pressed her mouth closed and nodded firmly. "I do. I really do."

"Well, then." Phil took his wallet out of the bottom of his Christmas bag and flipped through the old receipts and other miscellaneous slips of paper—what was all this mess anyway?—and pulled out the name and address. He held it out to Judith, and she took it between her fingers. Her eyes scanned the words, and then she looked at him, a question in her eyes.

"If you really, really mean it about that project, this little boy needs a bed."

He told her briefly about Cody at Kmart, and right off the bat she started wiping her eyes with her hands.

"A rag pile! Surely not!" she said.

"True as I'm sitting here," Phil said.

"Well, you just don't worry about a thing," Judith said, and tucked the slip of paper into her purse. "I'll take care of everything. I just can't imagine. . . can you believe it? The rag pile! Phil, I'm so glad I ran into you today. I needed something like this. Actually, I've been praying for something that would help me feel needed this holiday season. And here you were, and here it is!" She patted her purse and gave him a wink. "Why else would the Lord make me elf-sized if not to help Santa Claus complete his list!"

"Judith, you're a good one. God bless you," Phil said, and waved as she went to the check-out line.

Phil breathed out a sigh and felt a little bit lighter.

"Thank you," he whispered, glancing up. "Thank you for sending Judith to that little boy Cody."

Later at work, Phil turned the vacuum off and checked his watch. He had finished earlier than usual tonight. That's good.

"Hiya, Bishop. How's life in the real world?" he said to Brian Barnett, who stopped beside him.

"Ah, same old thing," Brian said. "Christmas is getting busier all the time." Brian was holding a briefcase in one hand, and his coat was draped over his other arm. "I tell you what, I feel like I want to lie down for a long winter's nap about now. I think bears have the right idea with that whole hibernation thing."

"It's only Tuesday," Phil said, and started winding the chord of the vacuum. "You got a long week ahead of you, buddy."

"Yeah, well, these kids put me through a lot by Tuesday," he said.

"That bad, huh? You'd think BYU students wouldn't get into too much trouble. But I'm sure there's more to bishoping than I care to know."

"It's not the trouble they're getting into." Brian put his briefcase down and pushed his arms into his coat. "I'm just getting buried in this whole Christmas thing."

"Buried?"

"Yeah. My Relief Society president had this idea to do a sub for Santa deal. We had the kids submit names of people they knew who were in need, and then we've just opened it up for donations. You won't believe the amount of stuff these kids came back with. My office is overflowing, my garage is overflowing, and my living room is overflowing. My wife's about to kill me."

Phil chuckled. He followed along beside Brian, and Brian waited while he locked the vacuum back into the custodial closet.

"So, you're off for the night?" Brian asked, and Phil nodded.

"Just finishing up. You?"

"Yep. I tell you, this year has been a humdinger. I thought things would slow down a bit as classes let out, but instead . . ." Brian shrugged.

They went up the stairs together. Phil opened the door, and a blast of cold air smacked into them. Brian waited while Phil locked up the building.

"I tell you, this giving out Christmas thing has been, well, the response has just been phenomenal. The kids are so excited they can hardly stand it."

"How do you plan on delivering it?" Phil asked.

"I haven't really figured that out yet. We'll probably do the typical knock and run deal."

"Well, Brian," Phil said after he thought about it for a moment, "how would you like to find out what happens when your Christmas is delivered to your families?"

Brian arched an eyebrow at him, and his forehead wrinkled.

"What do you have in mind?"

Phil gave him a grin. "Well, how would you like to have Santa Claus deliver your Christmas to your families?"

"That's a great idea—if we could get Santa Claus to deliver it for us."

"I think we can get that job done."

"Do you know someone who does Santa Claus?"

Phil grinned at him again. "You're looking at him."

Brian smiled. "And all this time here, I thought all you did was BYU custodial."

"Nah. Custodial is my job, but Santa Claus is what I do."

Phil pulled a card out of his breast pocket and handed it to Brian.

"Call me when you're ready, and I'll get those gifts delivered."

Brian called him by the end of the week.

"You up for this, Santa Claus?" he asked.

"You bet. What are we looking at?"

"Well, we have three, maybe four families in mind. One of them, well, all of them have some tricky situations at home. I'm not sure exactly how it will be received."

"I don't imagine I'll have any problems. I've learned that it's pretty hard to say no to Santa Claus."

"I guess you don't get chewed out so much in that suit as the rest of us."

"You'd be surprised," Phil said. "I've been cussed at, believe me."

Brian laughed. "By who? Who would cuss Santa Claus?"

"Well, there were these two ladies at Kmart this one year. I'd seen a bunch of kids already that day, and Kmart didn't cater to me too well. They gave me an old metal chair to sit on and took all the shelving off the racks, and I just sat up there, right on one of those racks. I'd been there about two and a half hours, and my old bottom was getting pretty sore, pretty tired of sitting there, so I decided to stand up and stretch out a little because there weren't any kids at the moment. So while I was standing there, these two little ladies rounded the corner. Now, I don't know if you've watched little old ladies shop, but they go down the aisle, and they paw absolutely everything and feel every piece of material.

" 'Oh, I wouldn't buy that, that's so cheap—Oh, but for that price it's not too bad.' That type of thing.

"So they're coming down toward me, and I thought to myself, 'I'm just going to stand there just as quiet as I can,' so I was standing there just being quiet.

" 'Oh, isn't that the cutest Santa Claus you've ever seen in your life?'

"And the other one said, 'Yeah, but I bet it's expensive as heck.'

"I couldn't resist any longer, so I said, 'I'm not all that expensive, ladies.'

"Well, I've been cussed at before, but never quite like that. I'm sure the rest of the customers in Kmart that day wondered what Santa Claus had done to those little old ladies. They just came unglued, totally unglued. They probably still don't like Santa Claus."

Phil grinned and finished his soda while he waited for Brian to stop laughing.

"You're lucky one of them didn't have coronary heart disease. You might have given her a heart attack, and she'd have sued you."

"Hmm," Phil grunted. "Lucky."

"All right, then," Brian said. "I'm thinking this Thursday night. We'll say around five o'clock?"

"You bet," Phil told him.

Phil parked in front of Brian's house right on the button at five o'clock Thursday evening. There were maybe a dozen or so students that helped him load up his truck.

"Well, Santa, you ready?"

"Ready or not," Phil said. His bells jangled as he packed the last of the packages into the back of his truck.

"What do we owe you for this?" Brian asked.

"Not a thing."

"Hey, there's still money leftover from the kids' donations. You should be compensated for your time."

"You can't pay me for experiences like this," Phil said.

"Your gas . . ."

Phil climbed into his truck and closed the door, leaning his elbow out the window.

"And how much did you donate to this project, Brian? Tell me honestly. How much of your own time, money, and resources?"

"Point taken."

"Good. Then I don't want to hear any more about it. Now give me the addresses."

Phil parked his truck in front of the house and turned off the ignition. He reached down, picked up his gold-rimmed glasses, and placed them on his nose. His smile came out, stretching out his white beard, and his eyes crinkled behind the glasses. He gave himself a "ho ho ho" into the rear view mirror, and then he was Santa Claus.

He got out and shouldered the first of the bags. It would take several trips back and forth to the door to get it all there. He walked quietly so his bells wouldn't give him away. When everything was on the porch, he gave three quick knocks.

Padding footsteps came from within, and then the doorknob rattled. A brown haired boy, maybe six-ish, opened the door. His eyes widened, and his mouth came open.

"Mommy! Mommy! It's Santa Claus! Santa Claus is at our door!"

The boy flew out of the room, shouting all the way, and Santa was left standing there, looking in at the empty living room. He chuckled.

The boy came tearing back in, dragging his mom behind him. A teenage sister came along, her face lit with a smile.

Brian had told him about the situation, the single mom with two children, and how the daughter had just had a baby.

"I have some things out here on the porch," Santa said. "If you don't mind, I'll just haul them on in, and you can help me put them under the tree. That okay, buddy?" he asked the boy, who was jumping from the couch to the chair and back again.

"Okay! Mom, he brought us presents!" The kid was cute. Freckled, sticky-up hair. Looked like he could have been in a Norman Rockwell painting.

Mom's eyes got wider and wider with every load they hauled in.

"The presents go there under the tree—that's a way," Santa said. "And these, well, we'll put these down here, and let Mom take care of them later." He set down three bags, all of them bulging with holiday goodies, including a full frozen turkey and all the trimmings.

"All right, then," Santa said after the last load was in the house and the door was shut behind them. "Come on over here," he said to the little boy. "Now you have to leave those presents there until Christmas." He chuckled. "Come right over here and climb up on my lap. I want to hear what you want for Christmas. What's your name, buddy?"

The kid was a wiggle a second. He was all over the place. Santa had to grab at his hat while he scrambled up onto his lap.

"I'm Henry Greer. I'm in third grade, and my teacher's Miss Ross."

"Well, Henry," Santa said. "What do you want for Christmas?"

"Well, I want a motorized scooter, like one of those ones the Prices have down the street. They go up and down the street, and back and forth, and I want to do that. I'll wear a helmet too, I promise, but you'll have to bring me one because I don't have one."

Santa shifted Henry's pointy elbow out of his ribs. He moved Henry around to the other side. He'd never seen a kid with so many bones.

"And I want one of those Heroscape games like Cameron has, with that one castle extension set. It's so cool. We play it at his house. I also want a new Game Boy, cause my old one broke, and I want . . ."

"Now, wait just a minute," Mom said. She was sitting on the couch across the room. Big sister had come too, holding the tiny bundle of her newborn baby.

"Wait just a minute, honey," Mom said again. "I think you need to look around here for a second. This isn't just some dumb old guy over at the mall. I think we've got the real Santa Claus here. Look at what he brought us."

Henry chewed on his fingers while he looked where his mother was pointing.

"He brought us food, and you know how we need food. And look," Mom said and pulled out a bag that was full of new clothes, neatly folded. "And he brought, looks like some clothes, and you know how we need that too. Do you remember how we need these things? How all your socks and pant legs have holes?"

"And he brought some other things too!" Henry said and bounced his way across Santa's lap.

"Yes, but do you see how careful he has been?" Mom asked. "To bring us just the right kinds of things?"

Henry looked from the grocery bags to the bag of clothes, and he stopped wiggling. His finger went to his lips. Even his eyes went still.

"Now, Santa Claus, ask him again what he wants for Christmas," Mom said.

"Okay, then, Henry. What do you really want for Christmas?"

Henry's finger pressed against his lips.

"Hmm," he said. "Hmm." He looked over at his sister. "Hmm. Well, you know my sister just had a baby."

"Yes, I know that she did," Santa answered.

"Well, she . . . the baby needs a dress so she can go to church and be blessed in."

Santa gave him a one-armed hug. "That's fine for Baby. Baby does need that. And what would you like for Christmas?"

"Hmm." Finger on the lower lip again. Henry's eyes went to his sister.

"My sister needs a pair of shoes," he said.

"She does need shoes," Santa said. "Okay, I think we could probably help out there. Now what would you like for Christmas?"

His eyes went to rest on Mom, whose eyes were smiling at her little guy.

"My mom needs a new dress," Henry said, smiling back at her. "Mom needs a pretty new dress for church."

"Okay, buddy," Santa said and nodded. "But what would you like for Christmas?"

Henry shrugged. "Oh, I just want everybody to be happy. That's all I want. I just want everybody to be happy."

Santa met Mom's eyes. They were shiny and wet with tears.

"I think we can take care of that too," he said.

The next house was brick, one of many matching saltbox units along a neat street. Brian had told him it belonged to a grandma and grandpa who had adopted their grandchildren when their daughter had lost them to the state due to drug use. They had saved for their retirement, and they would have had enough if it had just been the two of them, but to raise three more children . . . There was need here too.

Santa knocked on the door, standing among all the piles and stacks of presents and groceries. The door opened, and Grandma stood there, her mouth hanging open as she stared at his bright red suit against the white snow.

"I have some things here I needed to get delivered a little early," Santa said.

"But I . . . Are you sure? Do you have the right house?"

Santa took out the address.

"Three fifty-eight Sycamore Drive?"

"Well, yes," she said and opened the door a little wider. As he brought in the stuff, she stood there, gripping her hands and watching load after load hauled into her living room.

"Are you sure?" she asked again. "I mean, are you sure you have the right family?"

"Well, let's see," Santa said. He took out an envelope that was full of cash. He didn't know how much. Brian had handed it to him last of all. "Is this your name on the envelope?"

She took it between her fingers, and her eyes scanned the name.

"Yes. It is, but I . . . "

"Then open it."

She ran a finger along the top of the envelope, and her eyes got wide again. She flipped through the bills, her eyes growing wider and wider.

"Oh, my heavens," she said. She looked up at him, and there were tears in her eyes. "Who are you?"

He gave her a smile. "Well, as you can see, I'm Santa Claus. It's just what I do."

She went to him and wrapped her arms around him. Her hair smelled faintly of hairspray and dinner.

"Thank you," she whispered into his ear. "I don't know how you found out. I don't care how you found out. I just want to thank you." She pulled back and looked around at the stacks of packages and boxes. "I don't know who's doing this, but thank you."

4

Brian had asked him to come.

"I was wondering if you would come to a sacrament meeting the week before the students go home for Christmas."

"I could do that," Phil answered. "Except it wasn't Phil Porter that delivered the gifts. I get all confused in my head with Phil Porter reporting back. When I'm Santa Claus, I'm Santa Claus."

"Well, then," Brian said and paused. "Why don't you come as Santa Claus. Full costume. Full regalia."

So here he was, standing in the back foyer of the law building where Bishop Brian Barnett's ward met. The intermediate hymn was going right now. He'd already peeked in and had seen the entire stake presidency seated on the stand beside the bishopric. Had Brian invited them too? Phil rubbed a hand under his beard and started pacing again.

The hymn ended, and Brian got up to the microphone.

"Today we have a special guest to speak to us," he said, and Phil could hear the ripple of excitement that passed over the congregation. Great. Brian had connections in Salt Lake City. High connections. When he said they were going to have a special guest, it usually meant one of the Quorum of the Twelve. Phil took out his hanky and mopped his forehead.

"So I want you to welcome our next speaker . . ."

Phil started out onto the stand, and the congregation sucked in an audible gasp.

"Santa Claus!" he heard someone whisper. Loud.

"It's Santa Claus!"

"I think I'll just let him introduce himself," Brian said, and smiling, took his seat while Santa took the podium.

There were three girls sitting right there on the front row. Their whispers were not exactly quiet.

"What are they thinking? Santa Claus isn't supposed to be in sacrament meeting!"

Santa took a deep breath and started talking. Something happened then that he could never explain afterward. He talked to them about the giving of the gifts and about the unexplainable magic in selfless service. He told them about little Henry and how he had changed when he caught a glimpse of the giving the students had done for his family. He told them about the grandparents with their three grandchildren trying to make it on Social Security, and the way her face had changed and her eyes had spilled over with tears.

"Perhaps Santa Claus isn't real to everyone," he said. "But he becomes real when you give the way the Savior would have you give. Santa Claus is a symbol of Christmas, a symbol of Jesus Christ. My testimony of the Savior has grown stronger through the years as I serve him at Christmas time in this capacity.

"This year you have done something very special. For those families, for those children, it is everything. Remember how you feel now, having done that, and you will have learned the most important lesson Christmas has to offer. Christmas is about Jesus Christ. It is the time of year when people step outside of themselves, and they do things for other people, the way Christ spent his entire life in selfless service. So if you remember nothing else from this experience, remember this. If you do, you'll always have a very merry, very special Christmas for the rest of your life."

When he was done, he stood in the foyer alone, listening to the closing hymn. There was magic in the notes of "Silent Night." There were a great many snuffles and sniffs. His bells tinkled a little as he walked out the door. Maybe they heard them. Maybe not. But Phil was smiling now. Once more Santa Claus had done a job that in Phil's mind he should be doing: turning it all back onto the Savior Jesus Christ.

Later that night Phil got a phone call.

"Phil, I don't know how you do it," Brian said. "That was the most wonderful thing that has ever happened in my ward."

"Then they liked it?"

"Liked it!" Brian snorted a laugh. "But I have to tell you what the stake president had to say. As you left, after you shook the hands of all the bishopric and stake presidency, the stake president leaned over his counselor and my counselor and said, 'Bishop, I don't know where you got that guy. I don't know who he is, but that had to be the most wonderful Christmas program I have ever attended in my life.'"

Phil grunted but couldn't help the pleased smile that was splitting his face.

"Then he said, 'Don't ever do that again. The young sister over here is right. Santa Claus does not belong in sacrament meeting. But that was wonderful. Thank you for having this special Christmas guest.'"

"Well, that does it then," Phil said. "Next time, you speak."

Andrew was doing dishes at the sink when he got home.

"Hiya, Bug," Phil said.

"Hi, Dad."

"Hey, how was school? Denise, where's the mail? Has that package for Gina come yet?"

Denise was bent over her paints at the table, and she leaned her cheek into him for him to kiss.

"Haven't seen it," she said. "There's a sandwich in the fridge. Eat up quick. We only have about a half an hour before we have to go."

"Go?"

"Yes, Phil. Andrew has his school concert tonight. I told you about it last week. Twice."

"Denise, I . . . ," he glanced up at Andrew, who wasn't looking at them. His hands were scrubbing the pan, around and around and around.

He leaned closer into her and whispered in her ear.

"You know I have an appointment tonight. It's the Daniels' party. I do it every year."

"Phil, you already missed our family party . . ."

"Denise, please."

She turned away, dabbed the white paint along the edge of the ceramic figurine of an angel. Her brush clinked against the glass edge of the water jar, and the paint swirled out from the brush and clouded the water.

The clock ticked on the wall in the silence that hung between them.

"Phil, you have a family."

"Of course, I have a family! Why do you think I do this? We agreed—"

"We agreed that you would help supplement money for Christmas."

"And I am . . ."

"But that you wouldn't let it interfere with the family activities. Andrew's going to grow up and not have any memories of you being here with us during the holidays!"

"Denise, this isn't the time, " Phil said, snapping his mouth closed and huffing a breath out his nose. "Andy, let your mother finish those. You go on up to your room."

Andrew looked from one to the other. He took up the towel, and deliberately, slowly dried each of his hands. Then he tossed the towel onto the floor and brushed past them, knocking Phil's arm as he went by. Hard.

"Andrew!" Phil said. "Pick it up!"

His footsteps continued down the hall.

"Andrew!"

Now the footsteps were stomping, coming fast, thump-thumping along the hall. Andrew snatched the towel off the floor and almost ran from the room. His door slammed.

Denise put her paintbrush down with a solid tap against the table. She dried her hands and stood up.

Phil sighed.

"I'll go. I know. I'm sorry. I shouldn't have snapped. It's

just . . . You know how careful I've been." He shrugged. "I don't want him to know. He's so young still."

"Andrew doesn't understand why you miss everything. Someday you're going to have to tell him who Santa is. He's getting to be a big boy. He's already nine. Most kids his age already know that Santa's just a game. There comes a time when not knowing is worse. You need to come out of your little world and realize there's more to Christmas than Santa Claus. Do *you* know that Santa Claus is just a game?"

Phil blew out his breath. "Of course I do. Santa Claus isn't real in the same way Jesus Christ is real. I know Christ is the real reason for all of this. Santa Claus could never be put up on the same scale as that. It's just," he said, shrugging, "a game, like you said." Then he gave her a sheepish grin. "I just really like playing it."

"But what about Andrew?" she said quietly.

Phil pulled at the skin on his cheeks and chin. "It's just that I don't want to take it from him. There's something of childhood that is lost forever when a kid finds out about Santa Claus. I work every day trying to keep kids believing one year, even one day longer. I don't want Andy . . ."

"He needs to know something," Denise said.

"He's still so young," Phil argued.

Denise piled all her paints into the shoebox where she stored them. "Do you ever wonder if it's just us wanting to keep him young? He's our last. He's growing up fast, and we just don't want him to."

Phil pulled at his ear and shrugged one shoulder.

She nodded toward Andrew's closed bedroom door. "Go and talk to him."

Phil went to the sink, filled a cup with water, and drank it. He wiped his mouth on his hand and then walked past Denise into the hallway. The towel Andrew had picked up off the floor had been thrown purposefully down again, right in front of the bathroom door. Phil stooped and picked it up.

Outside Andrew's door, Phil knocked quietly. There was no answer. He pushed the door open, ignoring the boy smell that wafted up and seemed to come right out of the walls. Andrew's laundry was stacked to overflowing in one corner. His shoes sat crooked and upside down on the floor, and no less than seven pairs of dirty socks lay scattered all over around them. A bunch of toys and figurines stood up in fighting scenes along the windowsill, and Andrew's models were stacked in every other square inch of the room.

Andrew was lying on his stomach on his bed, his face buried in a comic book. The bed creaked as Phil sat down next to him. Andrew didn't look up.

"I'm sorry, Bug," Phil said. Andrew shrugged, and his eyes didn't leave the page.

"I know you heard Mom and I . . . I guess you figured it out that I'm not going to make it to your concert tonight."

Another shrug. "It doesn't matter. It's just a dumb concert."

Phil leaned over and took the comic book out of Andrew's hands. "But I hope you know that the Andy-bug who's singing in it is pretty important to me. I don't want to miss you. Or your big moment." Phil laughed a little and tussled Andrew's white-blond hair.

Shrug.

The silence settled in. Andrew shifted, and the bed creaked again.

"Dad, where do you go all the time? I mean at nights. You're never here after Thanksgiving."

Phil studied the pattern the dirty socks made against the tan carpet. He pulled in a breath and blew it out through puffed cheeks.

"I got—I have work."

Phil got up and brushed off his pants.

"One of these days," he said, "you're going to have to clean this room up."

"Yeah."

Phil touched a finger to Andrew's nose.

"I love you, Andy-bug," Phil said and handed him the towel he'd taken from the hall floor.

Andrew smiled and ducked his head.

When he was going to bed that night, Phil added another item to his list: "Talk to Andrew." Then he folded it and tucked it back inside his drawer.

5

Ruth Daniels met him at the door.

"Phil," she said. "We're doing something different this year for our party."

Phil steadied himself on the icy walk.

"Oops, don't slip there," Ruth said. "Roger! Come salt the walk! Now come on in here." She took Santa's arm and pulled him up the stairs and right into the living room. The whole room was stuffed with presents, stacked here and stacked there.

"Wow," Santa said.

Ruth smiled and patted at her hair. "As I was saying, we thought we'd do something different for our Christmas party this year. We wanted to give the children a chance to give to someone else. So we bought Christmas for someone who doesn't have as much as us. As you can see, so far, it's been quite a success. But here's where you come in. You know how I told you to come by a little early to get your bag loaded up?"

Santa looked down at his empty bag and then around at the stacks and stacks of presents all over the room. Ruth laughed.

"I guess what I should have said is come on over a little early, so we can load up your truck!"

"Uh-huh."

"See, the people we chose to give Christmas to, well, their daddy just got laid off. They have ten children, so you can see how the presents add up. So there you have it. Instead of sitting up on your lap and asking for what they want, the grandkids each chose a present for one of the children in this family—here's the address. And be careful going up that last hill by their house. It's a doozy in the winter time. Kids! Come in!" She raised her voice, calling into the next room. The kids started swarming in like bees.

"Santa! Santa Claus!"

"Hiya, Santa! You remember to bring me the Hot Wheels set?"

"Hey, there now, Brett! We're giving tonight, not asking," Ruth said with a pat on Brett's head.

Brett leaned into Santa. "Yeah, but you'll remember, right?"

The kids were scooping up stacks of presents and flooded out the door.

"Wait for me!" said little Abby from behind a big square wrapped box. She hurried out the door after them. They were throwing the presents into the back of the truck, one after another, and then running back into the house, grabbing up more, and back out again.

"Don't worry, none of them are fragile. We made sure. Now, here's the address," Ruth said, and patted her pockets, front and back. Santa held up a slip of paper. "Oh, I already gave it to you. Very good. All right then. The family is the Memmots, and their little girl, Kaylie, is Gloria's best friend at school, so that's how we heard about their troubles. Now you don't say anything to them about who—Candice! Get down from there before you break your head wide open!"

"Of course not," Santa said.

Ruth grabbed Santa's arm and started off toward his truck, hauling him along with her. "We're having hot chocolate and donuts after you get back, so come and tell us how it went."

Santa Claus sat for a minute in his truck, chuckling. He waited until they were all up on the front lawn before backing out. With a wave he turned the corner, glanced at the address, and went up six more blocks before taking the frontage road to the west end of town. He could hardly see behind him there were so many presents, just mounds of them.

He had a brief, quiet drive, sandwiched as it was between the Daniels' noisy brood and the Memmots' houseful. Ten kids adds up to a lot in a little bitty living room where the Christmas tree was glowing in front of the bay window. He set the Memmots to work bringing in the presents, and they dashed in and out and back again, squealing if they found their name on a gift. With that many helping, it didn't take any time at all.

"I can't believe it," Mrs. Memmot said. Her hand covered her cheek. "So much!"

Mr. Memmot shook his hand, and Santa Claus pretended not to see the emotion in his eyes.

Back at the Daniels' house, he shook his head to Ruth's insistence that he stay.

"I really ought to be going," Santa said. "Much as I love hot chocolate and donuts." He patted the padding in his suit.

"Oh, of course," Ruth said. "Thank you for your cooperation. This year's party has been funner than anything we've ever done. The kids even helped with the wrapping. I think we may be inclined to make all of it a good standing tradition!"

"Thank you for making me a part of it," Santa said, and Ruth gave him a hug before he climbed back into his truck.

"You're a good one, Phil Porter," she said.

"It's Santa Claus," he said, and gave her a grin and a wave as he drove off.

At the corner of Fourth and Main, he looked west toward his house and then east where Andrew's school was. He glanced at his watch and turned east. He smiled. The parking lot was still full. Maybe he hadn't missed it all. He quickly parked and was about to hop out when he caught a glimpse of his red sleeves.

Shoot. He couldn't go in there like this. He'd draw every eye in the crowd, and Andrew would run at him and yell, "Dad!" Everybody would see. Everyone would know. He leaned his head on his hand and sat there, looking in. At last he stuck the key back into the ignition and turned the engine back on.

"Sing your heart out, Andy-bug," Phil said, and turned back out of the lit parking lot into the dark street.

The next weekend, Phil was on the city corner again, waving

at cars as they went by. He kept the smile on his face, even after his arm felt like it was going to fall off. He'd had twelve honks in as many minutes, and most people waved back, but nobody seemed interested in stopping to talk to Santa Claus.

"Momma! There's Santa Claus!"

Santa turned. A little boy, maybe five or six, was tearing down the sidewalk, his mom, walking behind him, getting farther and farther behind. The boy plowed into Santa's legs—a full-on bear hug.

"Oh, Santa Claus! I love you!" the kid said.

Warmth just filled him. That one little thing made the rest of this cold day on the street corner in the city worth it.

"I love you too, buddy!" Santa said and hugged him back. "How're you doing today?"

"Oh, I'm good! I'm good!" he said. He went chattering on about the stores they'd been to and the bus ride into town, and Santa's eyes kept flicking to Mom, who was still catching up. Finally when Mom got close enough, Santa sat down on the bench, and the boy scrambled up onto his lap.

"What's your name, buddy?"

"Joel."

"Well, have you been a good boy this year?" Santa asked.

"Oh, I've been so good this year. I want—"

Mom cut right in. "Don't you tell him stories," she said. "Don't you tell him lies."

Joel's eyebrows furrowed as he looked back at his mom.

"I have been good. I've been really good!"

Her hands were on her hips. She'd probably had a good figure once, but age had settled her face into wrinkles and heaviness around her waist and hips.

"Don't you tell him lies," she said again. "He knows. He's Santa Claus. You can't lie to Santa Claus." Then she turned on Santa. "Ask him again," she said with her finger wagging in the air. "Ask him again, Santa. Just ask him."

Santa would have squirmed if Joel hadn't been sitting right on him. One thing he knew in this business is you don't get anywhere if you don't please the parents. He cleared his throat and patted the little guy on his back. Mom was searing a hole right through Santa with her glare.

"Okay." Santa cleared his throat again. "Okay, are you being a good boy?"

Joel's mouth was pressing tight together while he looked at his mom, but then he turned to Santa and his little eyebrows went up, wrinkling his forehead clear to his hairline.

"I have been good this year," he said.

Mom took two steps toward him, grabbed his arm, and almost yanked Joel right off Santa's lap.

"Don't you lie to him!" She was almost yelling. "Don't you tell him stories!"

Joel had tears in his eyes when he glanced back at Santa. His mouth was fighting a frown.

She came right up into her son's face. "Don't you lie to him, hear me?" She shook him by the collar.

Joel jerked away and slid off Santa's lap. His hands went to his hips in almost an identical pose that she was in.

"Momma! I have been good! Besides, I'm not the one who had to go to jail this year!"

Mom took a step back and seemed to shrink right up into herself. She pulled her purse over her shoulder, ducked her head, and walked quickly away. Her shoes clicked along the sidewalk until she turned the corner out of sight.

Then came Joel, right back up on Santa's lap.

"I have been good, you know, Santa Claus," he said once he was settled.

Santa tightened his arm around him. "I believe you." Santa's mouth kept quivering up into a smile, which was bound to turn into a full belly laugh if he didn't watch it.

"So, Joel. Tell me what you want for Christmas."

And Joel did. Santa waited until he too had disappeared around the corner before he let the laugh out. He was still breaking into chuckles a full hour later. Unbelievable.

6

A week later, Phil picked up the phone.

"Hello, Phil."

"Ruth Daniels. How are you?"

"You won't believe what happened. You know that family, the Memmots, we sent you to deliver to last week?"

Phil opened his mouth to answer, but she rushed right on.

"The thing is, they found out who it was all from. I'm sure little Gloria told her friend at school, and that was that, you know. And this is the neat part of it all."

"Uh-huh." Phil didn't need to say it. She hurried right along and never even heard him.

"I got a call last night and, you know, they are such cute people. They said it was all too much for them. So, bless their hearts, they said they know of another family that needs help this Christmas, so they took what they needed and want to give the rest to the other family. So what do you think? Do you want to do another delivery?"

He waited just a second before answering to see if she would really let him. "You bet. Tell me all about it."

It wasn't the sort of thing you said to a woman like Ruth Daniels, and Phil knew it the second it slipped out of his mouth. Ruth started in, and just for kicks, Phil timed her on his watch. Only took her twelve and a half minutes to get it all out, which, all considering, wasn't too bad really.

Mr. Memmot, whose name turned out to be Ryan, helped Phil make the next delivery. There were handshakes all around at the delivery house. Ryan was trying to blink away his tears again, but there was a light in his eyes that hadn't been there when Phil had delivered Christmas to the Memmot family.

"I can see why this whole Santa thing grows on you," he said.

"Yep," Santa said.

"I got laid off in August, you know. It's been almost five months."

Santa stared ahead at the road. He just nodded. Sometimes people just needed to talk and have someone willing to listen.

"It does something to you, being unemployed."

They drove for a minute, the sound of the engine filling the silence.

"One Saturday I went to the grocery store," Ryan said. "It was dark outside and pretty cold. There was a man sitting out there on the sidewalk, all curled up in his coat. He was holding a sign that said 'Need food. Please help.' Had a hat down on the ground. Didn't even look up when people walked by."

The yellow lines of the road slipped by beneath the thrum of the engine, and the lights on the houses flashed by.

Ryan cleared his throat. "When you came by, bringing all those gifts, part of me was so grateful. I can't explain what it feels like to know that Christmas is coming and your children are going to go without." Ryan's voice caught. "But part of me," he wiped a hand under his nose, "resented the sign you had put on me. A sign I didn't want to carry."

Phil reached up and took off his glasses. They made a soft clatter when he put them down on the dashboard.

He put both hands on the steering wheel and turned the corner until he pulled up in front of the Memmot's house.

"We've all had our ups and downs," Phil said. "I've been a police officer, a bus driver, a custodian, and a manager at a fast-food restaurant."

"Not to mention Santa Claus seasonally," Ryan said.

"I've seen a lot of things in my day," Phil said. "In fact, there was an experience in my earlier years that really . . . well, it was what turned me into Santa Claus. I had just started this thing but had been in it long enough to know I was good. People told me all the time, 'You're the best Santa Claus we've ever seen.' I was the most popular guy around. Everybody loved me. Santa Claus was like my alter ego, my hidden superpower. I'd done better financially than I'd thought I would. That year my goal was to pay back the money I'd spent on my costume, but I did that and then made an extra three hundred bucks. You bet I was feeling pretty fine.

"But then I got a call from Nancy Jordan and Millie Hair.

"Nancy says to me, 'Me and Millie Hair 'cross the street teamed up and want to give Christmas to a family. But, you know, this lady won't accept the gifts if they're coming from us, so I thought, how 'bout if we get Santa Claus to deliver them? And we want to remain anonymous. Do you do appointments like that?'

"And because I was Santa Claus and was so wonderful, I answered her, 'Well, I guess, since it's for charity, I guess I could do it for ten dollars.' "

Phil grunted and shook his head. "Can you believe that? I was so big-headed I figured I was giving her a bargain. But Nancy agreed. She says, 'Well, alrighty then,' and told me to come right over.

"I got there early, and they helped me load it all into the truck, and then I headed out, drove along the street twice where the address was before I realized that the big old house off the road, back just far enough to make it more impressive, was the one.

"I braked across the street and sat there, just looking at it. It couldn't be right. There was no way. I checked the address in my hand again, checked the address on the door, but I still couldn't believe it. The house was enormous, and not just enormous, but showy; you know, the kind that practically scream out 'there are rich people living here!'

"So I shifted into drive and away I went. Found a pay phone at the Fast Gas. 'Nancy,' I said, 'I think you maybe gave me the wrong address.'

" 'What is that, dear?' I admit she sounded a bit miffed at me.

" 'Well, it says Two-twenty Lakeview Drive. Two-twenty?'

'Yes. It's a big, nice home, and it sits back off the road a bit.'

" 'Uh-huh.'

" 'Well, then. Go on and deliver Christmas.' She almost hung up on me, she was that clipped.

"So I drove back. This time turned off the engine, but I still couldn't get out. The house was huge. Bigger than anything I ever hoped to live in. Curving brick driveway and wrought iron gate, all the amenities. What was this anyway? Me and Denise were tight in those days. Really tight. We were just scraping by trying to make it from paycheck to paycheck. And what were Nancy Jordan and Millie Hair, in their tiny, turn-of-the-century homes doing giving Christmas to people who lived in a house like this?

"Well, I delayed as much as I could, but there was nothing to be done but get on with it. So out I go to the front door with my biggest bag just stuffed full of presents. There were forty-two steps up that long, twisty walk to the front door. I still remember that. And the doorbell—it was one of those kinds that bongs all through the whole house. Even that doorbell sounded rich.

"So then came footsteps from the inside, and I stretched out my face into a smile, and started in.

" 'Ho ho ho! Merry Christmas.'

"From the kids it was the usual reaction. 'Santa Claus! Santa Claus!' They, four of them, were jumping around. Mom came around the corner, a slim, pretty woman, youngish. Her eyebrows went up, and then they drew together. She just stood there, very still, watching, and didn't even invite me into the house.

" 'Well, I have a few presents here . . .' I started, and the kids were bouncing all over the place, and she was just standing there, arms folded, looking at me. Not offering anything.

"So I said, 'I looked at my list and there you were, extra specially good. So I made it a point to deliver Christmas a little early.'

" 'Who are you?' the woman asked.

"I took hold of my suit right here on the fur collar and shook it so the bells rang. 'I'm Santa Claus,' I said. 'Who do you think?'

" 'All right kids,' she said loud enough to be heard over the top of their shouts. 'Go and get all these presents put under the tree. And then go on up to your rooms. Mommy's got to talk to Santa Claus for a while.'

"I admit I wasn't really wanting those kids to go. She just kept watching me, but after the kids were gone, her eyes filled up with tears and something else. I couldn't tell what. Not then.

" 'Who are you?' she asked me again."

Phil cringed as he remembered how he'd tugged at his beard and thumped at his chest. " 'I told you. I'm Santa Claus.'

"Her hands came up. 'No. No, no, no. You don't understand. Who are you really?'

" 'I'm Santa Claus.'

"Then she cussed me.

" 'I just want to know who you are and who's helping you,' she said after she'd run out of steam.

"I just wasn't getting it," Phil told Ryan. "I just die over it now, even after all these years, how proud I was.

" 'Well, my elves at the North Pole,' I told her.

"The tears fell down her cheeks now, but her eyes were hard and angry. Her words came out so full of emotion that they almost blasted me over.

" 'Apparently you're just some guy that's got a suit. You don't have any idea of anything that's happening here. I just want to thank whoever's behind this. You don't understand anything. You're probably even getting paid to do this.' "

It was his own words that came back to hit Phil the hardest. *Well, I guess, since it's for charity, I guess I could do it for ten dollars.* At the time, he had almost staggered under the blow . . . *Paid to do this . . .*

"I felt lightheaded from the shame, it was that palpable. I just stood there, couldn't look at her again, couldn't muster my Santa Claus smile. I felt like I was five years old and had just been spanked. She just stood there, watching me and letting the silence stretch longer and longer.

"Finally she said, 'Do you have a minute?'

"I looked up, and the hardness was gone around her eyes. Only the tears were left.

" 'Come in,' she said. 'Come have a seat in here with me.' "

Phil remembered how she had led him into the living room, where the Christmas tree sparkled above mounds of presents. The kids had piled them up haphazardly. Some had been stacked three high, big on top of little, but it had been a beautiful sight.

She had sat down across from him, crossed her legs, and folded her hands. Then she took a breath and let it out.

Phil narrated the rest of the story to Ryan.

The woman had spoken quietly. "Six months ago my husband called me on the phone from work. He said, 'I don't love you anymore. The divorce papers will be served to you this afternoon. I had to tell you before they came with the divorce papers. They told me I had to tell you.' He said he was going to marry his secretary as soon as this divorce was finalized." She had rubbed her pale hand across her cheek.

"I don't know what happened," she said. "We had a good marriage."

Phil recalled how this woman had sat there for a second, just real quiet. He had heard his own breathing and suspected that if he held his breath, he would hear the lights on the tree flash on and off.

"He told me I could keep the house, and we'd each keep the car that we drove. He wanted a clean break, no residual mess. So with the house, he said I got to pay the house payment—if I wanted to keep it." Then she had looked down at her hands. "It's a nice house," she continued. "I don't care about that, except it's the only home my children know. It comes with their school, their street, their friends, and neighbors. He took so much from them. Sometimes I get angry when I . . . Well, anyway, I try month by month to make the horrendous payment. It's been difficult." Her voice had caught then, and she swiped at her eyes.

"You probably noticed the For Sale sign on the lawn. I'll sell the house in a second, but I have to get enough out of it that I won't be drowning in debt. I don't know what I'd do . . ."

She took a deep breath.

"Do you see that room right there?" She pointed to the door on our right. "I have two sewing machines in there. I sew women's lingerie, and the ladies down in town let me put it in their shops. They don't even charge me a commission for what I sell, and in fact, they try to push my lingerie before they sell their other items."

The woman had sniffed and wiped a hand under her nose. "So far, I've been able to keep my head above water. I've scraped along, and I've made my house payment. And then Christmas came along."

Phil remembered how she had stopped. Her lips had trembled, and she had pressed her mouth closed, held a curled fist to it, and let out a deep breath.

"Basically we've eaten up our two years' supply of food in the last six months. But I've kept everything paid." She lifted a hand in a shrug. "I went to my bishop, and he told me that anybody who lives in a great big pretty house like this doesn't need any help."

At that moment, Phil had seen himself sitting out in front of her house, staring in at the obvious opulence. He would have dropped his eyes, but she had been looking at him—she would know that he'd had the very same thoughts.

The whole of the house, the whole of it, everything had faded around this woman. It was like the world had blacked out. All Phil saw was the woman sitting there, the heaviness in her eyes and hollow shadows in her face—these things had stood out harsh and stark, like the realities of life she'd had to carry.

It had been hard for him and Denise that year as well, and there were two of them, both working to carry the load that this woman bore alone. Even after all this time, telling the story again brought tears to Phil's eyes.

The woman had looked at Phil then. "The other night I was sitting in my bedroom and I was so depressed," she said. "And I didn't have any money, and I didn't have any presents for my kids. Well," her voice caught on a sob, "my twelve-year-old son came to me, sat down on the edge of my bed, and said, 'Mom, don't cry. Don't be sad for Christmas. It's a happy time of year. Don't worry about Christmas for me. Don't buy me any presents. Buy the little kids something. I'll help them play with their toys on Christmas morning, and I'll be happy. I don't need anything.'"

The tears had poured out of her eyes. Phil had blinked hard, and a big tear of his own had plopped right onto his nose.

"Here's a twelve-year-old boy that's willing to give up his Christmas because he knows that I don't have any money. And now look." She had pointed at the tree. "Look under the tree."

The presents, piled there by the kids, meant that there would be happiness for today, happiness in that house that had seen so much sadness. Phil had wiped his eyes again. He hadn't deserved to be a part of their little speck of happiness, but there he had been, and he was grateful for it.

The woman had again looked at Phil. "Now my twelve-year-old son will have a present to open on Christmas morning that won't be a pair of homemade pajamas or homemade underwear. There will be a toy for him to play with under the tree. I don't know who hired you, but I need to thank them. Do you see why I need to thank them?"

Phil remembered how he had brushed the fur on his pants down and stood up. It had been a minute before he could speak. "I have to thank you for setting me straight. And I want you to know that the love I see in your kids' eyes for this funny little suit and this silly beard is all the thanks that me and my elves need."

"Well, how can I repay you? Can't I . . . Can I give you a hug?"

Phil had smiled big. "Of course you can. A hug pays for a whole lot."

Then she had come over and given him a hug, just squeezed him tight. He patted her on the back, and she sniffed into his wig.

"I left the house a new person," he told Ryan. "I had to sit there in my sleigh for a while before I could see to drive. Then I went back to report what had happened to Nancy and Millie."

"Just as I had been ready to leave, Nancy went back to her bedroom and fussed around in her purse. She had waddled down the hall in her funny little walk, and I saw that a ten dollar bill was waving back and forth in her hand.

" 'Here's your money, Phil. Take your money. Come and get your money—don't forget your money.'

" 'I'm sorry. I can't take that money from you,' I said. She had stopped then, clutching the bill, and her mouth quirked up on one side, almost like the beginning of a smile.

" 'I know that Christmas is almost over with,' I said, 'and you won't have enough money to give someone else Christmas. But I got into this business for a reason, and if I take your money, my business will fail, and I won't be able to do what I want to do with what money I'm able to get.'

"Nancy had stood there, watching, that little smile playing at the tips of her lips. I kept going on. I had to say it.

" 'You see, I've been given a gift. My Heavenly Father has given me a gift that I can put a smile on people's faces, that I can spread a little bit of joy. If I can't spend a little bit of time giving for people like you, my gift will be taken away, and I will have failed in this portion of my life.' I curled Nancy's fingers around the bill.

" 'I don't want to fail, Nancy. So you take that money, and you put it in a safe place, and when you do Christmas again next year, you call me, and I'll make sure that your Christmas gets delivered.' "

Phil drew in a big breath. It shook a little coming in. He wiped a thumb at the wetness in his eyes. Ryan was staring straight ahead now. His eyes were on the empty ice-lined road, but his lips were pressed together, and a muscle quivered in his neck. When Phil finished talking, he turned and nodded.

"Thank you, Santa Claus," he said. "Now I understand. I know that you bringing us Christmas this year was more than just for my kids. I needed to hear that story tonight. It's funny how somebody else's problems always make yours seem easier."

"Yep. And one thing I've learned, there's always an end to every valley. Things will look up again soon. It feels like shame passing through the valleys of life, but there's no real growth without them."

Ryan held out his hand, and Phil shook it.

"Thank you," Ryan said. "Thanks for letting me come and help you do this. I needed to feel like I was on the giving end of things again."

"And now," Phil said, "you know and understand the magic of Santa Claus. It's my only secret."

7

Phil looked at the elbows of his costume and sighed. The fur was nearly worn through. How many years had it been now that he'd been wearing this suit? Ten? No, it was the year they first started asking him to come to Kmart. Twelve years! Unbelievable. He felt the worn fur along the seams and then studied the knees.

"It's getting bad, Mom, look at this," he said, and Phil's mom came over, peering over her glasses at the suit.

"Yes. Yes, you're right," she said. "Definitely time for another suit."

Phil sighed again.

"But how? Denise can't make it. Not at home. Not with Andrew . . ."

"Well, don't look at me for sympathy. Tell the boy already." She sat down on the edge of her spare room bed. "It's time you took all your stuff to your own house."

Phil glanced at her and then at the closet stuffed full of his Santa Claus stuff.

"It's getting more complicated all the time," Mom said. "You trying to sneak out in full costume in the middle of our Christmas Eve parties. And you know I want to have Minnie come in to spend a couple of months with me since she lost Harold this year."

"I know."

Mom sighed, sounding just like he had a minute ago. "Tell

him. You know you have to do it eventually. He's not a baby anymore."

Phil sighed. "It's like this, Mom. He's just at that age where
all he wants is to hold on to the magic of Christmas. Every kid by
his age kind of knows that Santa Claus can't possibly be real. Not
with the flying reindeer and all of that. Kids these days are far too
scientific for that." Phil grunted. "Too cynical too. They're on the
brink of losing that spark of childhood that they'll never ever have
again. If there's anything at all that I can do to give Andy one more
year of the magic, you bet I will."

"But don't you worry that one day, when he does find out, he'll
feel betrayed? Like you spent your whole life trying to find elabo-
rate ways to keep him believing something that just isn't true?"

Phil stood up. "But that's just it. I don't believe that Santa Claus
isn't true. You want me to sit down and tell him, 'Look, Andrew,
everything we've told you about this is a big fat lie'? No siree! Santa
Claus is as true and real as . . . as generosity and service . . . as real
as love. Those things are intangibles, but they're not a big fat lie
just because you can't see them—because you can't define them in
a scientific world. Santa Claus is the part of Christmas that allows
parents to give to their children in an anonymous way—the way
Christ would have us give. He's a personification of the Spirit of
Christmas, a symbol for Christ Himself. There's nothing about
that that is a lie!"

"Oh, all right." Mom hefted herself to her feet. "I should have
known better than to come head-to-head with you on this. And
stop all that pacing. You're making me nervous." She patted his
arm. "Well, anyway, I'm not worried. I know you'll think of something, some clever way to work through this so it won't spoil his
Christmas—for the rest of his life."

"I just remember how the magic went out of it for me when I
was about Andrew's age," Phil said. "It was such a letdown. I know
I need to get all this out of here." He waved in the direction of his
costume. "I understand that. I just . . . Let me think about it a few
more days. Something's bound to happen."

Mom let out a low chuckle as she dusted the shelves. "All part of your magic, right?" she asked. "You found it again, didn't you, the magic I mean." She turned and gave him a wink. "Round about the time you put that old Santa Claus suit on."

The doorbell rang, and she started out the room.

"Well, there it is," she said with another laugh. "Your magic."

He straightened his suit on the hanger and slipped it into the closet. It needed a cleaning too, but that could wait until after the Crandall party tonight. Mom was talking to someone at the door, and a minute later she called to him.

Phil went out and grinned.

"Jim Brekner!" he said. "How're you doing? How's your Santa Claus work holding out?"

"Up and down," Jim said. "Yours?"

"Couldn't be better."

"It's because you are Santa Claus," Jim said, and he turned to Phil's mom. "Phil is different than the rest of us," he said. "We put on the suit and play a part. He puts on the suit and really becomes the guy. You know, my kids have always been scared of Santa Claus, but when Phil did our party last year, well, they loved him. They fight about who gets to sit on his lap, hold his hand, ride piggy-back on him . . ."

Mom shrugged with her eyes at Phil. "Like I said. Magic." Then to Jim, "He actually lies awake at night thinking up ways to answer kids when they ask him difficult questions. Like the other day someone asked him if he wore a seal skin under his suit. Told Phil he wasn't the real Santa Claus if he didn't 'cause some kid had read in a book that the real Santa Claus wears a seal skin to keep warm. You know what Phil told him? He says, 'That's only true in the North Pole. It's so much colder there than here. If I tried to wear a seal skin here I'd just sit and sweat.' Then Phil hands the kid a candy cane and sends him off happy as could be."

Phil shrugged. "It just comes to me. Sometimes I lie awake thinking it over and wondering at how it all happens."

"See, I told you," Jim said. "The rest of us go to bed at night figuring out what's coming up at work the next day or how the refs called the game wrong, so our team lost the playoffs."

They laughed, and Phil shrugged.

"Can't help it," he said.

"Well, I'm glad you're here, Phil," Jim said. "I actually came by hoping you would be. I was wondering if you had a night when you could come Santa Claus for my kids again. They won't stop talking about the Santa Claus who came last year. I'll trade you the favor. I've got Tuesday or Thursday night free next week."

"Actually," Phil scratched his chin. "Actually, what I'd like better than that is . . ." He glanced at Mom and gave her a miniscule wink. "I was wondering if you'd come by as Santa Claus and ask Andrew if it would be okay if his daddy helped you out a bit. Tell him you need help, that you can't be everywhere at once like on Christmas Eve, and that you've got me trained up to be just like you. Stuff like that."

Jim nodded. "All right. You trying to break it to him slowly?"

"Mom's tired of me dressing up at her house."

"Ah. Well, then, it's a deal."

"Oh, and Jim," Phil said. "You gotta tell him that he's got to keep it secret. That's part of the deal. He can't be telling his friends. Make him promise."

Jim nodded. "Okay. I got it."

Phil thought it over on the way home. Was he naïve in thinking he could preserve this part of Christmas for Andrew? Would Andrew come to feel, as Mom had said, betrayed because Phil had tried to hold on to the magic for him so long?

"No," Phil said to the road. "No. He'll understand. Kids should come to know gradually, so they understand what it's all about. By then he'll know what Santa Claus's true place in Christmas was—serving the Savior. By then he'd know." Phil would help him to know. And it would have to be soon. Andrew was growing up. Much as he would like to, even Phil couldn't argue that. Nine years was old to still be a believer. But no way was he taking the magic away from his own son. No way.

Phil turned up Fourth North and waved at Sue Worthwright, who passed him in her car. Maybe he did put too much stock in the magic of Christmas, but he'd seen too much not to. Things had a way of coming together in the most extraordinary ways when he wore that old suit, things he could never explain. Like the night he told Cindy Crandall when her baby was going to come. Phil laughed out loud. That time he'd really set himself up. It was back in those early years when there weren't such things as ultrasounds for pregnant women. He'd been met at the door by Cindy, and she was just as pregnant as could be. Her sister Jackie was also at the party, and she was pregnant too, both of them just as round as you please.

"All right, you kids, you go on and finish putting your ginger-bread houses together," Cindy told the children. "Go on then. It's my turn to sit on Santa's lap. Come on, Jackie."

"Oh-ho! Ho, ho!" Santa said as each of them took a knee.

"Come on, Thomas, get the camera," Cindy ordered her husband.

"What do you want for Christmas?" Santa asked Jackie while Thomas flashed the camera at them.

"Well," she said and grinned at her sister. "I want a nice, healthy baby."

Santa pursed his lips and nodded. "Well, hmm. You're not quite ripe yet. You need to wait . . . oh, about two months."

Jackie laughed. "How did you know?" she said.

"Oh, Santa Claus knows everything," he told her. "Don't you remember that from when you were a little girl?"

"You know I'm not due until about February."

"Yep. That's what I thought. About two more months."

"My turn," Cindy said. "Enough with the pictures, please." She waved her husband away. Cindy's two little boys, respectively three and five years old, were giggling at them on the stairs.

"All right then, what do you want for Christmas?"

She put a hand on her round stomach and said, "I want this baby before Christmas." She gave him a look. "And I want a girl."

"Hmm," Santa said. He put a hand on her stomach and squinted his eyes. "Oh." He nodded. "Uh-huh. Hmm. Nope. No, you're going to have a boy, and it's going to be born early Christmas morning."

The smaller boy started hopping up and down, and the older one let out a whoop.

"Woo-hoo! Santa Claus says we get a little brother, and it's coming on Christmas!"

"Woo-hoo!" the little one echoed back.

Cindy groaned. "Not another boy! You've got to be kidding me! On Christmas Day!"

The boys were now running around the room, shooting at people and whooping like nobody's business.

"Now look what you did!" Cindy said, standing up with her hands on her hips while Jackie laughed. "What's going to happen if this baby doesn't come when you . . . ? The boys heard you say . . . ! Another boy!"

Santa gave his most solemn nod. "You're going to get a little boy on Christmas morning."

"You better be pulling my leg. I'll be so mad at you!"

Santa only smiled and went out the door with a wave and a jingle of his bells.

Phil flipped on the car radio to Christmas songs and chuckled at himself. That had been particularly brave of him, but he didn't regret it. He just knew these things. He'd always been right with his own children, even when the doctor insisted his second child was a girl. Phil had been adamant, and as it turned out, right.

And there it was, on Christmas morning, the phone call at 6 A.M.

"Merry Christmas," Phil had answered.

"Darn you, Santa Claus," Cindy had said into his ear.

"Oh, you got your baby, did you?"

"You were right," she said. "It's a boy. He was born about two o'clock this morning."

"What about your little boys? Do they know yet?"

"No. My husband hasn't woke them up yet. They're down at Grandma's house. I imagine they'll be up pretty soon."

"Well, congratulations."

"I still don't get it," Cindy said. "How did you know?"

Phil chuckled. "That," he had said, "is one of Santa's best kept secrets."

And now, well, even now he couldn't explain it. These things just happened. It was all part of the magic of Santa Claus.

Later that night he went to the Melburn's Drug Store business party. It was one of those jobs where the whole family was invited. Here came a little guy with his mom holding his hand. He looked at her, squinching his face up.

"Come on," she said. "It'll be fun. Just go talk to him."

The little boy pulled on her arm until she had to bend down next to his face.

"I don't want to," came the loud whisper.

"Just try," she said, and pushed him toward Santa Claus. He gave a little sigh and flumped onto Santa's lap.

"Hiya, buddy," Santa said.

"Hey." There wasn't anything like an answering smile. "My mom said you're one of Santa Claus's helpers, but I don't believe it at all. Are you the real guy or a fake?"

"Well, what do you think, buddy?" Santa met his scrutiny. The boy shrugged.

"I don't know."

"Well then, let's take a look," Santa said. "Take a look at my suit. Does my suit look like the real one to you?"

The boy turned his head and studied the suit from top to bottom.

"Yep."

Santa fingered the ends of his beard. "What about my beard?"

The boy stretched his neck one way and then the other, studying the beard.

"Come here," Santa whispered, leaning into him. "I'll let you pull on it."

His eyes widened. "You mean it? I can pull on your beard?"

"Yep. But don't pull too hard. That hurts."

He reached up a hand, paused, and then gave it a little tug.
"Ow!" Santa said.

The boy's hand covered his mouth. "Sorry," he said, while Santa scratched at the place he'd pulled.

"Now," said Santa, "what about my boots?" He stuck out a boot that was topped with the thick, beautiful fur from off the cuffs of his first suit. The boy reached down and touched a finger to the fur.

"Don't those look like real Santa Claus boots?"

"Yeah." The boy smiled. "The last guy I saw had some black plastic stuff over his feet, and his tennis shoes were hanging out underneath the plastic, like that." He drew a line along the top of his own foot to show Santa how it had been. "But yours look like real Santa Claus boots."

"Okay, then. Here's a candy cane."

The boy scrunched up his face again. "I don't like candy canes."

"Now wait a minute. Would I bring you a candy cane you didn't like? If I was a fake, well, then I might, but if I'm the real guy, wouldn't I bring you a candy cane that you really liked?"

Santa held out the candy cane, and the boy wrapped his fingers around it. He peeled down the wrapper and stuck it in his mouth.

"Hmm," he said. His cheeks sucked in. "Hmm."

"Well?" Santa Claus asked. "What do you think, buddy?"

He turned to his mom. "You lied to me. This isn't a Santa helper. This is the real guy!"

Phil laughed as the little boy skipped away, holding his mother's hand, and sucking that candy cane for all he was worth. That was what it was all about.

There was something about the little guy that reminded him . . . that was it. He saw himself as a little boy. He'd gone to Primary that day after school, and Santa Claus was there. There had been nothing quite like the excitement of that day. Afterward he'd run into his house yelling.

"Momma! Momma!"

She had hurried out of the kitchen, wiping her floury hands on her apron.

"What?"

"Momma! We had the real Santa Claus at Primary today!"

"No kidding! The real Santa Claus!" She put her hands on her hips. He remembered how she'd been smiling and had white flour streaks across the tummy of her apron. "How do you know?"

"Because he gave us candy canes that we all liked."

She pushed at a wisp of hair that was hanging down into her face.

"What do you mean?"

"Because we liked them! They weren't hot. And they were cherry flavored!"

Santa looked around, and since everybody was pretty much done coming to see him, he reached down into his bag and pulled out a candy cane. He peeled back the wrapper and stuck it into his mouth.

"Hmm," he said. "There it is." And he smiled.

8

Even though he knew it was coming, Phil jumped when the doorbell rang. He took a deep breath and held it.

"Andrew!" Denise called from the kitchen. "Andrew, honey, can you get that?"

Phil's heart picked up, and he started down the stairs, deliberately slow.

Andrew didn't look up from his comic book as he came toward the door. His hand fumbled on the doorknob, and then his comics fell with a slap to the ground.

"Santa Claus! Mom! Dad! Santa's at our door!"

"Well, what do you know," Phil said, giving Jim a miniscule wink. "Why don't you let him in."

"Umm . . . Come in," Andrew said to Jim, who entered in a jangle of bells. "I . . . uh . . . well . . ." Andrew shot a look at his mom who answered with a little shrug. "I don't know if you know it, Santa Claus, but Christmas isn't for another two weeks."

"Actually," Jim said, "I came just to talk to you, Andrew. Just to ask you a question."

"Really?" Andrew asked, his eyebrows raised high. "To me?"

"Come and sit down," Phil said, sitting himself down on one end of the couch. Jim took the other end, and Phil motioned a hand for Andrew to sit down between them. Andrew perched on the very edge of the couch, his feet set like he might spring up and run any minute.

"Andrew, I've been watching your dad," Jim said.

"Has he been naughty or nice?" Andrew asked and giggled behind his hand.

"Well, mostly nice, but actually I've had my eye on him for another reason. I need him to help me."

"At the North Pole?"

"No. Right here." Jim took a deep breath. "I guess you know I get pretty busy around this time of year."

"So does my dad," Andrew said.

"Yeah, I bet." Jim glanced at Phil and then went back to Andrew. "But, believe it or not, I'm even busier than your dad."

Andrew let out a grunting laugh. "Yeah," he said.

"So what I was thinking, after watching your dad, is that he'd be pretty good as one of my special helpers. You know I can't be everywhere all at the same time, and there are so many kids who want to see Santa Claus at Christmastime."

Andrew studied his shoes.

"I pick a few guys every year that I think can do a good job at it, and then I give them special training so they know how to be just like me. I even train them how to answer questions like they were me." Jim leaned in close to Andrew. "You know what? Your dad is the best I've ever seen. I think this will work really good, except," Jim leaned back and folded his arms, "I need to clear it with you. For a couple reasons. First, it means he'll have to spend a lot of time away from home, away from his family during the holidays."

Andrew shrugged. "Yeah, okay."

"And second, and maybe even more important, you have to keep this secret. You can't go off and tell your friends that the guy wearing the Santa suit is really your dad and not me. Do you see why that's important?"

Andrew glanced at Phil, his eyes scrunched up, and then back at Jim. "Yeah. Hey, I know now! This all came around last year when you," he pointed at Phil, "were driving a bus in Alaska! You must have taken a detour to the North Pole and gotten trained by Santa Claus! That's why you were gone so long!"

Phil exchanged looks with Jim and nodded his head. "That's good thinking, Andy-bug," Phil said.

"So what about it?" Jim asked. "You okay with this? Do you think you can handle the responsibility that comes with it? It's a pretty big job, and your dad's going to need your support."

Andrew lifted a hand, half-shrugged, scratched his head, and then laughed.

"Okay," he said.

"That was clever, Porter," Denise said after Jim had gone and Andrew was buried in his comic book again. She leaned in and kissed Phil's cheek.

"Thanks. It wasn't really me, but," he shrugged, "I'll take it."

"So when are you bringing all your stuff over?"

"I was thinking in the morning. Only problem is . . ."

"What?"

He sighed. "My suit ripped. Do you want to go over to Mom's with me and see if there's something we can do? It just has to get me through a week and a half . . ."

But Denise was already shaking her head.

"Is this another one of those frayed seams that wouldn't hold together with duct tape?"

"Hmm." Phil turned and studied a spider crawling up the wall. "I have the Harward party tomorrow night, and the Rudd family party Saturday night."

"Call Jim. Or Spencer. There's other guys in town who do Santa."

"Denise, I've done these family parties for twenty years. I can't let them down by sending another guy!"

"And you can't be Santa Claus without a costume. What do you think you'll wear? A pair of jeans and a windbreaker? Sorry, Phil, but I don't think even you could pull that off."

He blew out his breath. "Something will turn up. It always does."

"So you're not going to cancel your parties?"

"Of course not."

She shrugged and shook her head. "All right. You go and figure it out then."

The phone rang. Phil picked it up.

"Hello. Is this Phil Porter?" asked a voice.

"At your service."

"I hear you do Santa Claus."

"That's right." He turned away from Denise, who was making a face at him.

"Well, I was wondering if you were free Thursday night. It's my family's holiday get together, and well, we don't have a Santa Claus anymore. We asked Frank Jensen to do it, but . . ."

"Frank Jensen. I know Frank. He does a good Santa Claus."

"Well, he died last week."

"Oh. Oh. Well, you're right, he wouldn't be able to do Santa Claus for you then. Let me . . . check my calendar. I think . . . yep. Well, I'm free from seven-thirty on. If that will work for you."

"We can make that work."

Phil took down their name and information and hung up.

"Another party?" Denise asked.

"Yep."

"Did you tell them not to worry if you show up in your bathrobe?"

"Something will come up," Phil said.

"Okay. Something will come up."

"Frank Jensen died," he told her.

"Frank Jensen?"

Phil sat down at the kitchen table. "He's the one that got me started in this. Remember that guy that used to do the city parties? It was back when I was a police officer. I used to bring him down in the fire engine. You remember how tight we were in those days? Well, I got to talking to him, and he said I ought to look into being Santa Claus at people's parties. Said it supplemented his Christmas every year."

"I remember now," Denise said.

"Remember how I borrowed the city's suit that first year? Man, I can still smell that old thing! Musty old mothballs and dust."

"It had definitely seen some wear," Denise said with a laugh.

"I dressed up in that old thing and went around to the neighbors' houses and handed out candy canes."

"From that moment on, you were it. That's all it took to make you Santa Claus."

"That was the beginning, anyway," Phil said. "The very beginning."

Phil picked up a local paper and a donut at the Fast Gas. Then he followed the address on the scrap of paper. Frank's house was an old brick saltbox with a long, sloping driveway and juniper trees growing in a row along the fringes of his yard. Well-kept yard too.

Phil got out of his truck and stuffed his hands into his pockets. *What am I doing here anyway?*

Well, there was nothing for it, but to finish it up. He went to the door and knocked.

The phone book listed Frank's wife as Melva. She answered the door with a question on her face.

"Melva Jensen?" he asked, and she nodded, half-hiding behind the door.

He smiled, fumbling his keys in his pocket. Then he jerked his hand out to shake. "Hi. I'm Phil Porter. I know you don't know me, but I . . . well, I wanted to come by and tell you that I'm sorry for your loss."

The door came open three more inches.

"Thank you," she said. The lines around her mouth softened.

"I didn't know Frank very well, but for all that . . ." Phil shrugged. "Well, you could say he changed my life." She was just watching him, her eyebrows drawn together. "See," he said, "I do Santa Claus."

The door opened wide, and her face was smiling now.

"Oh!"

"Frank was, well, he was the reason I got into it. I used to watch how he just glowed for the kids at the city parties. He had a sparkle and a light in him."

"Yes, he did," she said. "He did. Won't you come in?"

Phil looked around, almost shrugged again, and then wiped his feet on the mat before stepping into the house.

"So, I guess you're here in answer to the ad?" Melva asked.

"I . . . uh . . . What ad was that?"

"Why, the Santa Claus suit, of course. I'm selling it all. The whole kit and caboodle." She squinted at him. "I see you need a beard. I'm afraid Frank grew his own. Whitened it with that old liquid shoe polish. He'd brush it in, and brush it and brush it until his beard was all white." She sighed. "Every year he used a little less shoe polish. He was getting whiter and whiter all on his own." She sniffed and touched a tissue at her eyes. "This last year, well, he wouldn't have had to use much shoe polish at all."

"You're . . . you're selling his costume?"

"Yes. All of it."

"Well, then," Phil said and nodded. "Well, let's take a look at it then. It so happens that mine is pretty worn through."

She led him into the kitchen where the suit, the padding, the hat, and the bags were folded in neat stacks along the table. He fingered the red fur. It still had a lot of wear in it.

"He always felt when he got into that costume that he really was Santa Claus," Melva said.

"I know exactly how that feels."

She was standing behind the chair, both of her hands resting on the back of it. Phil ran his hand across the white cuff and then looked up at her.

"What was his magic?"

"His magic? I don't know . . . What do you mean his magic?"

"Everybody who really gets into this has something that is magic to him," Phil said. "Something that turns him into Santa Claus. What was Frank's?"

She smiled a soft sort of smile, the kind that is made from a hundred thousand Christmas memories. Her eyes were focused on something far, far away, and they twinkled a little as she turned back to Phil.

"I think it was his bells. He never wore bells on his suit," she said. "He always had this leather thing that he had his bells on, and he'd always shake that thing and rattle it as he went into the house. He didn't like them on his suit, so he always carried his bells."

They stood there, smiling at each other, the Santa Claus suit resting between them.

"So, Mr. Porter . . ."

"Phil."

"What's your magic, Phil?"

He smiled. "My magic is my glasses."

"Your glasses?"

"You know, I don't know why. I think it's because . . . well, they're just special. I bought a pair of the little costume type glasses, the little square glasses with gold frames, and they didn't fit very well, and they were kind of uncomfortable. And they were impossible to see through. You could shine them up and polish them all the day long, but they were just impossible. Just poor glasses. Then one of the lenses came out, and I decided to go and get a new pair. I went to the costume shop, and they were all out. They sold them for five dollars, but you could rent them for two dollars and fifty cents a day. Well, I thought that was a bunch of baloney, so I went on to an optical shop. I asked, 'Have you got any Santa Claus glasses?' The guy gave me a funny look. I started looking, and I found a pair of reading glasses, just a pair of reading glasses, and they fit down over my nose, and they became my magic. They're the last thing I put on every time I get ready to go do a party, and I look in the mirror, give myself a jolly 'ho ho ho,' and away I go."

Melva reached over and patted his hand.

"Very good," she said with a smile. "It's too bad you didn't get to know Frank better. You two would have gotten along well. He would have liked you, Phil." She stood up and opened a plastic container full of cookies. She gave him one with a napkin and poured two glasses of milk.

"I've heard Santa Claus really knows how to enjoy a good glass of milk and cookies," she said. The cookies were deep, rich chocolate with tiny peppermint chips in them. His was gone in two bites flat.

"So your glasses became your magic," she said.

"It's what turns me into Santa Claus. And it's funny how I see things differently through them. I see the good in people—I want to see the good in people when I look through them." He took a sip of his milk. "There was one time I forgot my glasses, and I knew it as soon as I got out of the car. I knew right away I'd forgot my glasses. I didn't have my magic. Nothing felt right. Good thing I only had one appointment that night, because I was just off the whole night."

She took a tiny bite of her cookie and dabbed her mouth with her napkin. Her eyes were smiling at him.

"You make a lot of memories through the years with this Santa Claus thing, don't you?" she asked. "One of the things Frank did was to get an elf costume for the grandkids. I made it for him. When the grandkids get to be ten-ish—big enough to fit the suit—they get to go out with Grandpa and be Santa Claus's elf. They stand beside him and take the packages out of the bag and help him give them to the kids. Ronnie is almost twelve, but he's small for his age. He was supposed to be Grandpa's elf this year, but Grandpa got the cancer in October, and . . ." She shrugged her shoulders. "He was looking forward to it because he could finally fit into the elf costume—he had to wait an extra year, you know. It's such a letdown for that child."

Phil leaned toward her. "Well, give him something of Grandpa's Christmas magic. These!" Phil said, holding up the fur-lined boots. There's no way they'd fit him. They looked no bigger than a child's.

Melva's mouth came open. Then she smiled, and her eyes sparkled with tears.

"I'm so glad I like you," she said. "I don't think I could give Frank's costume over to someone I didn't like, but I can tell you're the right one. He would want it that way. In a way I can think of you as his successor."

"And I couldn't ask for a better example," Phil said. He looked the costume over, examined the padding. "It's perfect. I'll take everything—except the boots of course." He picked one of them up. It was eensy. Size seven or something. He could no way stuff his size eleven foot into that. He handed them back to her, and she cradled them to her chest while he wrote out a check.

He stacked it all up in his arms. At the door one of the velvet bags flopped halfway off the pile. Something heavy inside of it banged against his leg.

"Oh. Wait. Wait, there's something in here." He felt inside the fabric and took out a line of bells strung on a thick leather circlet. He held it in his hands, feeling the weight of the bells and running his fingers over the worn, stained leather. Then he put them into Melva's hands.

"I know why you're selling this stuff," he said. "I know why you're getting rid of it. Because you can't stand it. And I know when that time comes in my house, my wife will do the same thing. But please, keep his magic. Keep his bells, and next year, hang them on the door, so that any time the door opens, you'll know that the magic is still here, so that Frank can be a part of you and a part of your Christmas every year."

"Oh dear, you are Santa Claus," Melva said with a hand to her cheek. "You feel this even more than Frank did, I think." She leaned up and gave him a squeezing hug. "You go on and wear that suit. I'll feel that part of him is still alive because you're out there doing what he loved—Frank's legacy will live on because you're still helping children in his costume."

Phil put a hand on the doorknob, and as he opened it, said, "I will do my best. I promise you I'll do my best."

The next day, Phil found the newspaper in the front seat of his truck. Oh, yeah. He'd picked it up with the donut yesterday. He tucked it under his arm and opened the door.

"Hey, Mom."

She looked up from the recipe box, her fingers flip-flipping through the cards.

"Ah! There you are."

"Came to get my Santa stuff. I found another suit."

"Good! And while you're here you can help me decide whether to do bacon-wrapped chestnuts or spinach dip on Christmas Eve. Have a treat."

He sat down and grabbed what looked like some kind of caramel layer bar.

"Braileys brought those by last night," she was saying. "The first was delicious, but the second was too rich. Go on and take the rest home."

He flipped open the paper and scanned the headlines. He gasped.

"What?" she asked.

He slapped the paper down onto the table and pointed.

"Teenager dead from reckless driving," Mom read aloud. Her finger came up, tracking her eyes along the words.

"Jack Taylor." She squinted up at him. "Do you know him?"

"He's . . . well, I've been doing the Taylor family Christmas party for fifteen years. I've known Jack since he was yea-high." Phil gestured with his hand to his hip.

She sat back, her eyes shaping concern. "I'm sorry, Phil."

"I'm scheduled to do their party again this year. On the twenty-fourth. Christmas Eve. I guess I better call Debbie and Travis and see if we're still on. It's just . . . how do you make that kind of call?"

Jack Taylor was dead? It made Phil's head spin around a confusion of sadness. How could someone so young and full of life be suddenly wiped out of life? How could parents cope with losing a child right before Christmas like this?

That night he took out his list. He crossed off "Talk to Andrew" and "Find a new suit." Two big ones done. His hand paused over the paper, and then he wrote, "Call the Taylors." He sat for a long time staring at the list, wondering what in the world he would say.

As it turned out, he didn't have to make the call. Travis's mother, Hannah, called him the following night.

"You know the sadness that we have right now," she said. Her voice was scratchy, like it had been dragged across the rough surface of sadness. "You know about Jack's death. Even though none of us feel up to it, we're going to go ahead and do our party on the twenty-fourth, same as every year. We have to hold up a sense of normalcy for the little ones."

"Of course," he said.

"Well, we bought a picture that we want to give to Jack's mother. And we want you to do that first. I'll get the picture and give it to you, and you can give it to Debbie."

Phil's stomach clenched up into a knot. "Oh no," he said. "No, don't do that to me. It would . . ." He could just see how that would set the tone for the party. "Look. Do you trust me?"

"Do I . . . What do you mean?"

"Do you trust me? Will you let me do it my way?"

"Well. What is your way?"

"Let me do it my way. There's a chance we can save your Christmas party."

There was silence for a minute on the other line, and then Hannah let out a tired sigh. "Well. All right. I'll trust you. Whatever you do is fine with me."

"Then you have the picture ready, and when it's time, I'll gesture to you and you can bring it out."

"Okay. Good-bye, Phil."

When he hung up, he held the phone to his forehead.

"Oh, man." It came out like a groan. "Dear Father in Heaven. Please help me with this one."

Denise blew in through the door in a blast of cold air.

"Whew! It's cold out there!" she said, and dropped her load of shopping bags onto the table.

"You won't believe what I . . . what's the matter?"

Phil blew his breath out through his lips. "Well, Jack Taylor died in an automobile accident."

She opened her mouth. Her cheeks were cute and red from the cold.

"Is that the kid who was in the newspaper? I read about that! Barb said the friend was traveling too fast, the one that's still in the hospital in critical condition. I guess the one that was killed, Jack, had had a fight with his mother before he left with his friend. His mom said she didn't want Jack to go with the friend because he scared her. That friend always drove too fast. Jack promised he wouldn't, and then last minute went with the friend and ended up dead."

Denise blew on her hands and rubbed them together hard.

"They went screaming down the freeway going like a hundred miles an hour, and the car flipped and killed the one kid."

"Jack Taylor," he filled in.

"Yeah."

"Well, I'm going to do their family party on Christmas Eve."

Her eyes almost made him break down and bawl. "Oh, Phil."

"I know."

She took off her coat and flopped it over the back of the chair.

"But look what I found. Not those," she said, taking the bag full of lotion and perfumey soap out of his hands. "Those are for the girls at Bunko." She pulled out a plain brown paper bag and pulled out a big wad of newspaper. It had little strips of shredded newspaper hanging off here and there.

"I was at the ceramic store, and I found the neatest thing." Her hands stripped off the newspaper as she talked. "The minute I saw it I knew. I said, 'I need to get that for Phil.'"

She held a figurine of Santa Claus kneeling in front of the manger where Baby Jesus was. It was raw white ceramic, and it was the most beautiful thing he'd ever seen.

"Oh, wow!" He took it from her. "I love it. I'm going to paint it right now."

"You paint it?" She laughed. "I thought you had a party tonight."

"It's not until six thirty."

"You really want to paint it? I figured I would, and—"

"No, no. I really want to. I took an art class in high school.

It's been a while, but . . ." Phil shrugged. "It's something you never forget. Like riding a bike."

"Well," she said, but he was already back out of the laundry room with a handful of brushes in one hand and her box of paints in the other.

He squeezed out dabs of color onto the pallet. He started right in on the red coat, but the cheery red straight out of the tube was too bright. It almost looked orange against the stark white of the ceramic. His other choices were maroon, fuschia, or raw sienna, which was really an orange-ish brown. He mixed in a dab of this and that.

"Aha," he said. That was it. It took a little dab of cherry red, a bit of maroon, and a little bigger dab of the sienna. It was perfect. It was just the color of his first suit. Now that was a beautiful suit. He'd never had another one like it.

He painted the back of the ceramic Santa Claus's coat. The ceramic was textured to look like fur, and it made the red come alive. Such a vibrant color, red. It was one of the things he loved most about Christmas. Maybe it was the symbolism of it, the reminder that Christmas was really about Christ, his life, and his ultimate sacrifice. Red was Phil's favorite color. If he didn't know better, he'd say it was part of the magic. Like the one year he'd done Christmas Eve for his boss over at BYU. Mike had about eight kids, ranging from twelve to a little baby. They had several acres of property, and on Christmas Eve, they'd build a fire, drag out all the benches and chairs to set around it, and Mike would tell the story of the Nativity. Then they'd all pile up into their Ford Bronco and drive from one end of the property to the other. The whole thing was supposed to represent the journey that Joseph and Mary took.

The deal was that Phil was supposed to flash the lights in his truck at Mike so he'd know he was there, and then Mike loaded everyone up into the Bronco. Phil had to hike down to the fire, the equivalent of several city blocks. The snow had been deep that year; it was up to his calves and sometimes clear to his knees. He could still remember how good that fire felt when he finally got to it.

The sky had been clear. The full moon reflected off the snow. The air had this crystalline kind of mist, like all the moisture had frozen into minute specks of ice that sparkled and shimmered like . . . well, like magic. He saw the Bronco coming toward him. He remembered stepping behind the fire then. Later, Mike said it was the most unbelievable thing he'd ever seen.

He said that the light of the fire caught the red of the suit and projected it up into that mist so that there was a huge, shining, scarlet *V* over the top of him.

"We could see you perfectly," Mike said. "Your white beard and your red suit, the firelight and the frost in the air, and it just created this *V* that illuminated the whole sky. It was this glowing aura that shone clear to heaven."

Unbelievable!

The family came busting back over the bumps in the snow, their heads banging around inside the Bronco, just packed in there. They piled out, and their eyes were as big as saucers.

"Santa Claus!"

"Santa! Santa!"

The clear, shrill voices of the kids were like ice popping.

"Santa Claus! Where's your sleigh?" asked one little guy. He had freckles all over his face.

"Well, it's right up over there on the mountain," he said. And then he'd seen it. It was an airplane, just peaking the top of the hill, the little red light blink-blinking away. There it was, right where he'd pointed. "Oh, dear. You can see it, can't you?" He lifted his wrist to his mouth and made a crackling pop sound in his throat. "Rudolph, would you hide behind that tree or turn off your nose, whatever it takes. I can see you down here." And the airplane went over the side of the hill, gone the same second. It was perfect.

"Thanks, Rudolph," he said into his wrist.

The kids just went nuts.

Phil chuckled. Those kids were probably still believers to this day. He rinsed his paintbrush, turning the water a swirling pink. He rinsed it again and again, and finally it was clean enough to start the white. But again, the white was too stark, too . . . plain to paint on the cuffs and trim of the coat. He dabbed a bit of yellow here and there, but it looked like snow some dog had got to. He tried some watered-down blue here and there, but now it looked like mold growing on old leftovers in the fridge.

"Denise!" he called, and she came tramping down the hall.

"Oh," she said, peering over his shoulder. "You don't want that much color in the white. Rub it down, then paint over it with plain white, and let it dry. Sometimes it looks different dry."

Phil went at it, rubbing at the white parts until they were a greenish-grayish mess. Then he splatted plain white over the top and put the thing away, slid it clear back on the highest shelf in the laundry room, so he couldn't see it any more. With a disgusted grunt, he went out and got ready for his party.

9

"Now when it's time to go to bed on Christmas Eve, don't fuss about it, even if Mom and Dad tell you to go to bed a little early," Santa said to the kids staring up at him. "You see, I deliver presents to the good kids first, and I know you're all good kids. When I fly over in my sleigh, and I see you're still awake, I'll have to fly to someone else's house, and you know, before long, the night gets mighty busy for me. I just might not have time to get back to your house."

The kids sucked in their gasps. Little Maggie wrinkled up her nose.

"So when Mom and Dad say time for bed, you go, and go right in and go to sleep. Okay?"

"Okay!" they chorused back,

"Excuse me, Santa Claus."

It was a soft voice. Santa looked up to see a young lady. She looked like a teenager, but he knew she'd been married over a year now. He'd gotten her wedding announcement a year ago last April. She was holding a tiny baby.

"I was wondering," she said and held the baby out to him. "I was wondering if you would . . . I mean if I could take a picture of you with my baby?"

Santa held out his hands, already smiling. What a darling, teensy thing. It still had the red puckered look of a newborn.

"Well, of course, you can," he said, cuddling the baby to him.

He held the blanket back from the baby's face while she clipped a couple of shots.

"Now I've got one for you," he said, and he took the baby and turned it around, holding it up. He turned his back to the camera so that the baby's face was showing, looking down into his face. It made a real cute picture that had been popular with a lot of moms through the years.

"Oh," she said, smiling as she took a few more pictures. "I like that. But . . . " She fumbled in her purse. "But I like the first one better, the one where you were holding her. I like that one best." She pulled something out of her purse. It was another picture. She held it out to him.

"Look," she said.

He took it, looking it over. It was him. Years ago, in his first Santa Claus suit—Man, he loved that suit!—and he was holding a baby just like the pictures they'd just taken. He looked up at her.

"Well, I know who Santa Claus is, but who's the baby?" he asked.

She pointed a tentative finger. "That was me."

He gasped.

"When I was one day old."

His mouth was still open. "I remember that."

"Oh no, you do not, you can't . . . "

"I remember that." He looked past her where her mom watched them. "Mom, now Grandma, you'll remember this. We were on the east side of Provo, and I don't know whose house it was, but it was a little, tiny house. Everybody was crowding in because it was such a little house. Kids were sitting on top of each other all over the floor, and the adults were sitting all over the furniture, anywhere they could find. Some were standing in the kitchen doorway, and you went out and got the baby to bring in, and all the kids said, 'Oh, I want to hold it! Can I hold it?' And you wouldn't let them because she was only one day old. I was the only one you let hold the baby that day."

"He does remember it," said one of the younger men on the couch. "I was there. I was only five years old, and I remember Santa Claus holding Emily."

"I can't believe it," said Grandma. "How can you possibly remember that?"

Santa shrugged a smile. "I was the only one, with the exception Mom, now Grandma, that got to hold her that night." He smiled at Emily, and handed her back the picture. "Thank you for showing me that."

Emily reached out and took the baby from his arms. She put it to her shoulder and patted its little round back.

"Thank you, Santa Claus. Thank you for being part of our lives," she said.

Denise was wrapping presents when Phil got home.

"Hi." He leaned in and pecked her cheek.

"Andrew was asking about things again tonight," she said.

"Oh? Asking what?"

" 'Has Dad been doing this other years? Is that why we've never seen him at our Christmas parties? How come he doesn't do Christmas parties for our family? If he gets to be an official Santa Claus helper, how come I never get to see him do it? Can't I tell Jackson? I promise I won't tell anyone else. Can't I go with him on one of his appointments?' Let's see," she said and looked pointedly at him. "Did I miss anything?"

Phil kicked his shoes off, and let the sigh come out. "All right. I'll go talk to him."

"Your mom called too."

"Okay."

"She said she needs her spare room cleaned out by Friday because her friend is coming in from Seattle for the holiday."

"Okay. Did you have a nice evening?"

She rubbed her eyes. "I'm tired. Why is it that Christmas does this to parents? I still have six neighbor treats to make and deliver, that potluck dinner at Lucy's tomorrow night, endless wrapping, a lesson for Sunday to pull together, and I still don't know what I'm going to get for Lynn's family."

"I thought you'd decided on one of those games at that new store downtown."

Denise shrugged. "I didn't see anything that grabbed me. Do you know what's hardest about Christmas? It's the expectations. We all think it should be this fabulous, almost magical experience. We want to give our kids just the right thing, like if we don't, they'll somehow think we don't love them enough. It's so much pressure. And after we spend too much money and work ourselves to total exhaustion, we have to somehow convince the kids that none of that matters, because Jesus is the real reason for everything. How do we even do that? I feel like . . . I don't know. I just want it to be over."

Phil turned her around and wrapped his arms around her. He moved his hands over her neck, kneading the tension out from between her shoulders. She sagged against him, sighing.

"Mmmm. That feels good."

"I'm sorry I'm gone so much. I know this is hard for you," he said into her hair.

"I sometimes just really hate Christmas. Do you think I'm a Scrooge for saying that?"

Phil laughed. "Maybe a little. You got to put it into context who you're talking to."

"Yeah. Santa Claus." Denise laughed and kissed him and then patted his cheek.

"Go talk to Andrew. I didn't know what to say to him."

The hall light was still on. Andrew was nine years old, but he was no way going to sleep without the light coming in from the hall.

Phil stood for a second in the doorway, looking at the shadows of his cluttered room. The boy smell wafted up. What was that smell? Dirty socks, smelly shoes, clothes he'd worn and stuffed under his bed? Or the apple core and half eaten gingerbread man in his garbage? All of it was magnified by the heat pouring out through the heat vent.

Andrew was still, his white-blond head half-hidden under his blankets, burrowed in. That kid slept under fifteen blankets—didn't call it a good night unless he woke up in a puddle of sweat.

Andrew was too still to be asleep. He was waiting. It was some game he played, to see if his dad would actually come into the room and kiss him good night.

Phil did.

"Hi, Dad." Andrew grinned up at him. "Did you do good? Was it fun being Santa Claus?"

"Yeah, buddy, it's a lot of fun."

Andrew sat up. "I been thinking. Why don't we have everybody come over, all the cousins and grandkids, on Christmas Eve, and you can be Santa Claus, and let all the little kids sit up on your lap."

"I don't . . . Andrew, I can't."

"Why?"

"Well, they'd recognize me. They'd hear it in my voice that it was me. What if I slipped and called Kaitlyn 'princess'? She'd figure out it was her grandpa talking, not Santa Claus. Remember we can't let anyone else know about this. Even Jackson."

"Hmmm." Andrew's eyebrows creased a vertical line above his nose. "But I still wish . . ." He pouted his lips out. "I want to do it with you."

Phil leaned in close to him. "Tell you what," he said. "What if you ask your teacher about Santa Claus coming to visit your class on Friday?"

"You mean it, Dad?" There was the smile that Phil loved. He remembered holding Andrew in the hospital, the day he was born. He'd been . . . a surprise . . . coming thirteen years after their youngest child. They'd thought they were done, but here came this tiny, living, breathing thing. Phil had forgotten what it felt like to hold his own newborn child. It was like the blood in his veins had been replaced with pure love.

By then, he knew how the love kept growing and growing. Andrew was his fifth, after all, but every day there was something else, something so clever that this baby did, something that every other baby in the world had done, but it had never been this baby. And that was the miracle of it.

Phil could still remember the first time Andrew had smiled, laughed really. They'd just pulled up to the cafeteria where Phil was working early morning breakfast prep, and Denise had tickled that tiny little baby right in the tummy. Andrew had squirmed and giggled. That smile, that giggle, well even now, with Andrew's teeth too big and a little crooked, and his hair all sticking out, it just melted his old dad.

"Dad?" Andrew prompted, and Phil shook himself out of the memory.

"You bet," he said. "You ask your teacher, and tomorrow, say, around ten o'clock, I'll come into your classroom as Santa Claus, and we'll hand out candy canes. Does that sound like a deal?"

"Okay." Andrew jumped onto him, nearly bowling him right off the bed.

"Oof!" Phil caught him around the middle and wrestled him down, gave him a good tickle, and hugged him. "All right, now get back into bed and go to sleep, or I'll put a boot in your butt. How's that for a deal?"

Andrew laughed and snuggled in.

"Okay."

Phil was almost to the door.

"Hey, Dad?"

"Yeah?"

"I think it's cool you get to be Santa Claus."

"Yeah. It's pretty cool."

Phil was awake by five thirty. He lay staring up at the texture patterns of the ceiling. Jack Taylor was buried yesterday. Sixteen years old.

Finally Phil got up and went downstairs. The house was dark. Quiet. It used to be that the kids were up by now, all of them hustling in and out of the bathroom, grabbing a piece of toast, and shuffling through, trying to get last minute homework done. Back when the house was full of kids.

Phil's bare feet creaked on the floor as he went to the laundry room and took down the ceramic Santa Claus figurine. He squirted paint onto the pallet and stirred it around with his brush, added yellow and brown, a touch of green here and there, and worked on the hay in the manger.

A bed creaked down the hall, and he froze, but then all was

quiet again. Andrew usually didn't wake up until seven thirty. The clocked ticked quietly on the wall. How was it that all the other kids had grown up and now had kids of their own? Now it was just Andrew here with him and Denise. Where had all the time gone? Andrew was already in fourth grade. Phil had seen that when he visited Andrew's class yesterday. Kids that age all had the same sort of look, lanky, a little awkward, and those funny too-big teeth in their heads.

But there was nothing like the simple joys of that age. Phil had gone in and handed out candy canes just like he'd promised, the last day of school before Christmas. Andrew's smile had stretched as wide as the moon to see his old dad come in as Santa Claus. His whole face literally glowed. On his way out the door, Andrew had given him two thumbs up. It had shot straight to his heart and stuck there like a lump of pure gold. Kids were what made it all worth it. What would Christmas be without them?

Phil got a drink at the sink and wiped a hand down his face. He stood there, his hands resting on the counter, staring at the floor. Were Debbie and Travis Taylor thinking about the things that used to make Jack smile at Christmas? Did they see his smile in their minds every time they closed their eyes? What would they do with all the presents they'd already bought for him? How was anyone safe when such a thing could happen at any given moment? Phil shook his head. Would they still set a place for him at the Christmas dinner table? Still hang his stocking? Would they fill it?

Phil shook his head. He had to stop thinking like this. It left a hole that was too big, too wide, and too raw to imagine. How could they bear it?

Phil went back to the table and took up the paintbrush again. He studied the swaddling clothes and blankets that he'd painted last night after everyone had gone to bed. The whole of it was starting to come alive. Every time he worked on it, it stirred something deep inside of him.

He had finished the face of Baby Jesus, just a tiny bit of pink and peach, a dab of light brown for the hair. Such a tiny little thing to have so much, so very much significance. Enough significance to heal the hurt the Taylors were going through, to get them through their loss now, and one day, to make it right again.

Now he started in on the face of Santa Claus. His eyes were closed like he was praying, and the eyebrows showed his deep reverence and love for the baby he served. Phil knew what was happening here. It was more than simple worship. Santa Claus had received a call, and he was accepting on his knees, overwhelmed by the trust that had been put on him. He would go there often, often during his service, times when he needed help, when the needs of the children were more than he could fill.

Like tonight.

Phil closed his eyes, his gut clenching up. "Heavenly Father. Please be with me. Please comfort Jack's family. Please let me be thy instrument . . ."

The phone rang at noon. Phil had only just come in the door from making deliveries for Denise, picking up the last minute fixings for Christmas dinner the next day, and a quick run to the store for more wrapping paper and tape.

"Phil, will you get the . . ."

Andrew ran though, howling, his feet thumping the floor.

"Andrew! I can't hear your mom. What?"

"Get the cherry bars out of the oven, please!"

The phone kept ringing. He grabbed the receiver, tucked it under his chin, shoved a hand inside a mitt, and pulled the bars out in a blast of cherry-filled heat.

"Hello!"

"Phil. It's Judith."

"Judith . . . Oh! Hey!"

"I need to you come right over. We have just come back from delivering the bed to your little friend from Kmart. You need to come here and hear the story."

Denise was mouthing something to him. He covered the receiver.

"What?"

"I need you to finish up some shopping. I have three things left for you-know-whose stocking."

He nodded at her and then talked into the phone. "What? Now?"

"I know you must be busy, but you, well, you need to hear it."

"I'd love to," he said, and Denise gave him a look. He grinned, shrugged. "I will. I'll be right there. Or . . ." He shrugged at Denise. "I'll do my best." He hung up and caught Denise into a hug. She pushed against him.

"Porter, don't you get fresh with me! I'm busy! I don't have time to . . ." But Denise couldn't talk with Phil kissing her smack on the lips.

"I'll take care of it," he said. He was exuberant. Ecstatic. He danced a jig. "Make me the list, and I'll get it done. Denise, Judith just delivered the bed!"

She shoved him away, half laughing, and put a hand to her hair. "Okay. Oh, I'm glad. I'm glad." She nodded her head toward the door. "Go on. Do what you have to do."

He squeezed her. "I love you. You know that, don't you?"

His hand was on the doorknob when she called him back.

"Phil, the list."

He took it from her hand and dashed out the door.

Phil opened the door of his truck, pulled himself in, and nearly jumped out of his skin.

"Andrew! What are you doing here?"

Andrew was curled up on the floor of the passenger side. He looked up and grinned.

"I want to go, Dad."

"Andrew . . ."

"You're doing Santa Claus stuff again, aren't you? I want to come too. I think, and Mom would probably agree with me, you know, that I ought to go with you on some of your Santa Claus outings. You're my dad first before you're Santa Claus, so it's only right that I have a share in it. Right? How else will I have any memories of my dad at Christmas?"

Phil just sat there looking at him. What was he supposed to say? Then he laughed.

"Very funny, Bug. You have this all figured out, don't you? You know just what to say to get the old man's guilt going. Must have got that from your mom."

"So? Can I go?"

Phil huffed out another laugh. Then he shrugged.

"Okay. But I have to drop you back off before I take care of your mother's list."

"Deal!"

Andrew hopped up onto the seat and stretched the seat belt across his front, snapping the buckle in.

"Okay. Now here's what we need to do . . . Wait." Andrew turned to face Phil. "If this is Santa Claus stuff, shouldn't you be dressed up? I mean, how am I supposed to get a real feel for what you do if you're wearing blue jeans and that old T-shirt?"

Phil laughed and shrugged again. "All right then, buddy. I'll humor you. Because it's Christmas Eve. But you know you can't come with me tonight."

"Of course not," Andrew said. "Come with Santa Claus on Christmas Eve? Even I know better than that. Hey, bring your candy canes!"

Phil rushed back into the house, answered Denise's questions with a hurried shrug, and stuffed himself into his suit. Andrew was still sitting just as he had been, seat belt and all. Phil laughed at the way his eyes lit up when he saw him in the suit. And there was that smile again.

His bells jingled as they got out of the truck in front of Judith's house. Andrew hadn't reached to hold his dad's hand for, well a long time, but here it was, slipping into his palm. Phil practically skipped up to the door.

"Let me," Andrew said, and pushed the doorbell. A dog exploded in barks on the inside.

"Well, here you are!" Judith said, her face gushing smiles. "And don't we make a pair! Quiet, Maisy!"

Judith was dressed in an elf costume, complete with bells on her curled shoes.

"I figure since you've been calling me elf since grade school, and since the part fit most especially, it was time to dress the part. Oh, that dog! Quiet, Maisy!"

"Unbelievable!" Phil said, laughing. "It's fantastic!"

"You want to hear unbelievable? Come on in. Is this your boy?"

Phil introduced them, and she gushed over Andrew until they were settled in the living room. Maisy came after them, stiff-legged, and still barking to wake up the whole neighborhood.

"She's a good old dog," Judith's husband said from the recliner. "But so full of arthritis she can hardly move."

Phil fished in his bag and brought out a candy cane.

"Here you go, Maisy," he said, and handed it down to her. "Maybe this will keep you happy."

She took her candy cane to her pillow in the corner, flumped down on it, and started working at the wrapper.

"Now, Phil, you've met my husband, Bruce. Bruce, this is Phil Porter. He's Santa Claus."

"I see that," Bruce said with a crooked sort of grin.

Judith hugged her hands together. "It's been such an experience," she said. "I want to thank you for letting me help you in this. The whole of it from start to finish has been so fun. Everybody at the plant got involved."

Judith settled herself onto the couch across from him, her shoulders and hands waggling like Maisy's tail over her candy cane.

"Does your son know about the little boy from Kmart?"

Phil told Andrew about it briefly, just as it had happened.

"Does he really sleep on the rag pile?" Andrew asked. "How come his parents don't get him a bed?"

"Sometimes parents can't afford to buy all the things their kids need," Phil said. "You see that kind of thing a lot, especially at Christmastime."

"His parents are too poor," Judith said. "You should have seen that house! I could practically see the sky through the holes in the ceiling." She shook her head. "And such a passel of kids! It was a little bitty house. They must have slept six to a room. I never saw anything like it. But I'm getting ahead of myself. Maisy, don't choke on that wrapper."

The dog was having a time trying to get the wrapper off, so Phil knelt down beside her pillow. He pulled the wrapper off and tucked it into his pocket. That old dog put that candy into her mouth and sucked it—didn't crunch it down, but just sucked on it like a baby. Andrew got the giggles and sat beside her, resting his hand on her head.

"That spoiled old beastie," Bruce said from his chair. "If you pay her any mind she'll want to go home with you and sleep with you in your bed."

"And you're a lucky boy to have a bed," Judith said to Andrew. "I've just been visiting a little boy who didn't have even that."

She patted the cushion beneath her arm. "My brother made the bed. I knew he had the wood, and it wouldn't be a big deal for him, so I put my mind to figuring out how to get the bedding together. The first thing I did was to enlist my boss down at the sewing plant."

Judith alternated between him and Andrew. "Well, Ted—that's my boss—let me pick out the material for the sheets, pillow cases, blankets, and bedspread. Then I gathered some of the girls I work with—Meredith, Grace, and Susan were the main helpers, but nearly everybody put some time in on this. You should have seen the joy of it spread. Everybody wanted to do something. Even some of the men sat right down and helped us with the quilting.

"Well, Ted said we could only work on the project one hour before work and one hour after, and we made good progress. I was sure we would make it when I got a phone call from Ted two days ago. He said they were shutting the plant down one day early for the holidays. But we weren't done. We were close, but not done. So he says, 'Now I probably shouldn't do this, but I'll let you and your people work on this today during regular work hours because that little boy has got to have his bed.' "

Judith dabbed at her eyes. "I never saw anything like it," she said. "Ted is just a hard old man, grumpy as all get out. But you could see he had caught the spirit of this thing, and he was going to see it finished to the end."

Maisy hefted herself off the pillow and labored to her feet, walking crooked and stiff to Phil. She put her head on his knee, pushed her wet nose up against his hand, and her eyes asked clear as day for another candy cane.

"Well, there," he said, and patted her head. "Do you want another one? Let's ask Dad if we can. Is it okay if we have another one, Dad?"

Maisy looked over at Bruce, just meek as you please.

"You've had too much candy already," Bruce told her. "You can't have any more."

Her head went down, and she slouched back to her pillow and collapsed down on it with a big doggy sigh.

"Now, never you mind her," Judith told Andrew. "She's as spoiled a creature as you'll ever find. She wants you to think she's never had a lick of love in all her born days."

Andrew leaned his face down beside Maisy's and rubbed her ears. She let out another sigh, and Andrew giggled again.

"So I took Jake and Bruce with me—of course, I can't heft and assemble the bed. You've met Jake, my son. He just got back from his mission."

"Yes, I think I've met him," Phil said.

"He's a big boy," Judith told Andrew. "Just like you'll be in a few years. This little boy we were bringing the bed to, well, he wasn't big. Not even as big as you. Just a thin little runt. Probably never had a full meal in his whole life. I'd called his parents before hand so they knew we were coming, and that little guy met us at the door. His eyes were this big." She showed how big with her hands. "And his smile was just . . . well, he was just beaming. We set up the bed right over the place where his old rag pile was in the corner, and spread it with the sheets, blankets, and finally made it up with the quilt. It was pretty as a picture. I told him I was one of Santa Claus's elves, and I was delivering his present a little early because Santa wouldn't have time to set it up, to make sure it was just right and all of that. Besides, I said, we wanted it to be right in his own special corner, right over his rag pile, so that he would know especially that it was for him. And Santa surely couldn't do that without waking him up tonight. Do you know what he told me? He said, 'I knew Santa would bring me a bed because he said so. I saw a lot of Santa Clauses, but I only asked for a bed from the one I knew was real.' "

"That's 'cause my dad is trained by the real Santa Claus," Andrew said.

"Of course, he is," Judith said. "And little Cody could tell. And then, just as we were leaving—" She blinked fast as tears pooled up in her eyes. "Just as we were leaving, that little boy started pushing that big old bed out from the wall. His mama said, 'Son, what are you doing? That's your own new bed. You can sleep in it right there.' " Judith sniffed. "And do you know what that little boy said? He said, 'Uh-uh Mama, I can't sleep in my new bed.' And she says, 'But son, it's your bed,' but he just keeps shaking his head. 'No Mama, I can't sleep in my new bed. Not yet. Because Santa Claus hasn't brought the presents for the rest of the kids, and so I'm going to sleep on the rag pile, and I'm going to pretend that I didn't get my present yet so the other kids won't feel bad. Then tomorrow night, when it's Christmas, and everybody else is happy too, then I can sleep in my bed.' "

Andrew came up beside Phil's chair and laid his head on his shoulder. Phil slipped a hand around him and squeezed.

"Thank you, Judith," Phil told her. "Thank you for sharing that with me. Thank you."

"You needed to know," Judith said. "Besides, it's part of an elf's job to report back to Santa Claus."

They were headed out the door, and Maisy's feet thumped along behind them, her claws clicking against the tile in the entryway. Judith gave them each a hug, and Andrew leaned down and gave Maisy a good pat. She whimpered and looked up at Phil with such sad eyes.

He glanced at Judith and then at the family room where Bruce was watching the television. Then he dug in his bag and pulled out another candy cane. He unwrapped it and then held it down where Maisy could reach it. Her tail wagged three times in the air, and she took that thing up with her lips, didn't even touch her teeth to it, and trotted, happy as you please back to her corner.

Phil turned back to Judith and gave her a little shrug. "Merry Christmas," he told her.

"And merry Christmas to you," Judith said, with a twinkle in her eye and a wink.

"I liked that, Dad," Andrew said when they were both back in the truck. "I thought it was neat the way that boy got a bed. He didn't even have a bed, and she . . . and you . . . Do you do those kinds of things a lot? Give kids things?"

Phil tousled Andrew's hair. "It's what being Santa Claus is all about," he said. "Giving. It's what I like best about being Santa Claus."

"And you have elves and everything!"

Phil laughed. "Judith makes a good little elf, doesn't she?"

Andrew was looking out the window where it had started to snow, light tiny flakes drifting softly down through the cold. Andrew was silent all the way home, but his lips turned up in a smile as he watched the silent snow.

10

❄ ❄ ❄

Phil pulled onto his street at ten minutes past four. It had taken him two and a half hours to buy the three items from Denise's list. Between the crowds and traffic, shopping had eaten his day. He pulled to a rolling stop, and whistling along to Karen Carpenter, pressed the gas and moved out into the intersection. There were cars parked along both sides of the street, which probably accounted for why he didn't see it. There was a flash of movement caught in his periphery, just as his tires hit ice.

The child was wearing a helmet. It was bright red against the snow, and so close to his car he couldn't even see the bike. Phil shouted something, his foot slamming down on the brake. His back tires slid sideways. His voice rose to almost a scream. Was that a thud? The bump of a tiny body against the hard metal of his truck? The sound of his own voice choked in his throat. The snow was falling again, tiny, hard chips, landing with staccato ticks against his windshield. Finally the truck slid sideways to a stop, his brakes screeching. He jumped out, heart thundering. His hand touched the freezing metal of the truck as he pushed off and dashed around to the other side. The breath left him in a whoosh of relief.

The child's bike wobbled on training wheels, the girl's little legs pumping hard, whole and well. The pink tassels on her handlebars fluttered as she bumped up over the curb of the opposite street and safely onto the sidewalk. Phil leaned against the hood of his truck, his legs suddenly weak. He might have killed her, might have sent her crushed body to the hospital, and left her parents torn and bereft. He might have caused that anguish.

Phil bowed his head.

"Father, thank you. I can't imagine . . . thank you—"

She had been right there, his truck almost on top of her. It might have been the ice that grabbed his tires and pulled him back from the damage that would have taken her life and would have broken his.

"Thank you."

He wiped his eyes with his hand, and carefully, so very carefully, moved the truck out of park and rolled the rest of the way home, leaning forward, watchful.

He caught Denise up into a hug when he got home, burying his face in her hair.

"Did you get it? You got everything? What's the matter?" She pulled back out of his tight embrace.

"I almost hit a child in the truck. It was so close. I might have brushed her with the bumper. It was right out there on the corner. I might have killed her."

Denise touched a hand to his cheek.

"Oh, Phil. I'm so glad it didn't, that you didn't—"

"Me too. It was the grace of God that kept that child safe."

"Thank heaven," she said, and then pulled back again. "Where's the bag? You did finish the list? I've got to hide it before Andrew comes in."

"Left it in the truck," Phil said. "I'll get it." He went back, got the bag, and carried it to their bedroom. Denise was still in the kitchen. He could hear her puttering around. It might be his only chance.

He took out the present he'd selected for her. It was a small thing, tenderly chosen. The tiny box fit in the palm of his hand. With his thumb he flipped open the lid, revealing the small silver ring with a sparkling pink gem. What had the jeweler called it? Ah, well, he couldn't remember. It was pink, and pink was Denise's favorite color. She would love this little token to remind her how much he loved her.

He pulled out the wrapping paper but scrambled the contents of her craft box, the top drawer of his desk, and the bedside table drawer before he found the tape set out beside the scissors where Denise must have been wrapping earlier.

"Of course," he muttered, and bent to his wrapping. It was a clumsy effort, but he whistled as he went. He so loved Christmas. He finished it off with a bright red bow. When he'd finished, he stashed it back in his drawer until later.

His heart lighter, he returned to the kitchen, pulling in the aroma of Denise's clam chowder that would join the other crocks of soup at Mom's house tonight for the family party. He would make it there by the end, right before dessert and present exchange. He would be there with his own family to share that part of Christmas Eve night.

Denise was up to her elbows in suds and dishwater at the sink.

"Leave those," he said. "They can be done later. Who wants to do dishes on Christmas Eve?"

"Better now than Christmas Day," she said. "Besides, my mom always told us that Santa Claus never comes to a dirty house."

"Oh, he does," Phil said. "Believe me." He'd personally dropped presents off at quite a few homes that went way beyond messy.

"Where's Andrew?" Phil asked, picking up the dish towel and wiping it across the pan set upside down in the dish drainer.

"In his room, I think. Must be buried in some comic book again." She raised her voice, "Andrew!"

Phil stacked the pan in the cupboard. She called him again.

"Maybe he fell asleep." She toweled off her hands and started down the hall. Phil dried another pan, looking up when she reentered the kitchen.

"He's not there." She leaned over and studied the backyard through the window and then went to the front door and opened it.

"Andrew!" Phil called down the stairs. He could hear the TV on, but nobody was there. He walked down and flipped it off, and the silence that it left filled the house. "Andrew?"

His boots creaked on the stairs as he went back up. Denise was pounding the buttons on the phone.

"Kalli. Hi. It's Denise. I was wondering if you've seen Andrew. Is he over playing with Jackson?" She paused, her fingers drumming on the counter. "No?" Her knuckles passed over her mouth. "You haven't seen him at all? No, no. Everything's all right. Thanks."

She hung up and her eyes met Phil's.

"He's around here somewhere. Of course he is."

Phil glanced at the window. It was late afternoon, and already growing dark, and getting colder by the minute.

"Is his bike in the garage?" Phil asked, and they both dashed to the side door. The bike was gone.

"Phil—"

"I'll take the truck out," he said, snatching his coat from the hook and already moving out the door. Once around the block, Phil flipped on his headlights. How in the heck did it get dark so blasted fast? He turned on his windshield wipers, a senseless attempt to see more clearly. It was hardly snowing, a few solitary flakes. He flipped on his brights, scanning the streets.

In broad daylight, he had not seen that little girl on her bike. Where was Andrew? What distracted driver was passing along beside his little bike, unseeing? Or following him intentionally . . .

How long has Andrew been gone? His stomach knotted.

Phil leaned forward on the steering wheel, his eyes swiveling as he made a wider circle around the block. He rolled down the window.

"Andrew!"

Maybe he should do what the doc said and get his eyes tested. He couldn't see a thing.

He couldn't have come this far. Andrew knew he wasn't to go past Fourth North. Certainly not past Main Street.

Phil paused at the corner, turned around, searched the road

behind him, and then pulled out onto the busy road, filled with people rushing about their holiday.

"Don't panic, Phil. It'll be all right. He's around. Close." It was easier to believe when he said the words out loud.

He rubbed a hand under his nose. The blaring headlights made it impossible to see past the oncoming cars. Up ahead the lights of the grocery store revealed the parking lot jammed with last minute shoppers. His heart squeezed his chest, as he scanned the rows of cars, all of them pulling in and backing out with reckless abandon.

"Father, help me find Andrew," Phil said through clenched teeth. His hand touched his cell phone that would surely ring any second with Denise saying she'd found him. He took it off his hip and clutched it in his hand.

He was at the storefront now, inching along between pedestrians that were dashing in and out of the open front doors when he saw him. A burst of sweat flooded out his relief as he jammed the truck in park and jumped out.

"Andrew!" Phil shouted, and his son looked up at him, his face blossoming into a huge smile.

"Hi, Dad! Come and help! Look what I'm doing!"

Phil caught him into a hug, squeezing his little body. He kissed the top of his head.

Andrew had a bulging pillowcase slung over his shoulder, and he had on a pair of old green sweats, and Lynn's old green scout socks pulled up to his knees. He'd tucked the bottom of the sweats into the striped red tops of the socks, and his boots over the top of that.

"This is Kesler," Andrew said, looking at the man ringing a bell outside the store. "He's from the army."

"Salvation Army," Kesler said with a crooked-toothed grin at Phil. "This little man is trying to help me out here."

"He's gathering things for the poor people," Andrew said. "And so am I!"

"I've been worried, Andrew. Don't you leave without telling us where you're going. What is it?"

Andrew put the pillowcase down on the ground, and it clunked against the cement. "I've been helping the poor people. Like you do Dad."

"Andrew . . ."

His little boy cheeks were bright red from the cold, and his nose could have rivaled Rudolph's.

"I went to all the houses on our street, and all the ones on the other street—and look what I've got!" Andrew pulled open his sack and tucked his head inside, shuffling around in the contents. He came out holding a can of soup in one hand and a small packaged toy in the other.

"They're for poor kids! Like Cody! Who won't have Christmas!"

"Andrew—I've got to call your mother. She's so worried. We're both so worried. We didn't know where you'd gone."

"But Dad, I was helping poor people. You know you're not supposed to tell anyone when you do that. That's why I got in my elf costume."

"You're elf costume?" Phil rubbed a hand down his face.

Kesler laughed and tousled Andrew's hair.

"He's a character," Kesler said. "Look at him! Collected a whole bag of food and things. If everyone would do that, I wouldn't have to stand out here and ring a bell."

"You're freezing!" Phil caught Andrew's small hands and rubbed them together inside his own. "Come on, we've got to get you home."

"But wait! My sack!"

"I've got it, kid," Kesler said. "I'll make sure it gets to the right place."

Phil hefted Andrew's bike into the back of the truck and turned the heater on full blast as they headed back home.

"So I thought, since I want to grow up to be Santa Claus too, I'd better get practicing. That nice lady Judith told us about that little boy Cody, and I thought he's not the only little kid who is poor and needs help. My teacher in school at Thanksgiving said we would bring food for the homeless people, and so I took my bag and I—"

"Andrew, you can't be doing this." Phil's voice was harder than he meant it to be. It was because he was angry at himself. Somehow he had caused this. "You left without telling Mom where you were. You could have been run over or kidnapped. Do you know how many crazies there are out there?"

"But I . . ."

They could see the house now, and Denise was running down the driveway, watching them take the corner. She pulled Andrew from the car, crushing him against her. Tears streamed down her face.

"How could you do that?" Denise asked. "You know better than to leave on your bike. We were so worried. I called everybody, and then I called the police."

"You did?" Andrew's eyes were wide.

"We didn't know where you were! It's dark and cold! Honey, do you know how many kids disappear in America every year?"

"But I . . ." his voice caught, and he looked back over his shoulder at Phil.

"Let's get him inside. He's freezing," Phil said. He placed a hand behind Andrew's shoulders, guiding him into the house.

Denise took off his coat.

"What is this?" she said looking at his outfit for the first time. Andrew was wearing an old red T-shirt he'd worn when he was six. It had a faded Christmas tree on the front with a company's name emblazoned on the back. The bottom of it didn't even touch the top of his old sweats.

"It's his elf costume," Phil said.

"What?"

Phil drew in a breath. He felt like he was confessing crime.

"He was out asking for cans of food, toys, and other things for the homeless shelter. He was trying to be like me."

Denise's eyes still creased with confusion.

"Remember, he went with me this morning to hear about the bed for that little boy. He was trying to be an elf."

"Oh." Denise hugged Andrew again, rubbing her hands hard along his arms. "You silly, silly thing. You know you need to tell us before you go somewhere."

"I just wanted to be like Dad. He gets to be Santa Claus." The tears spilled down his cheeks, and his mouth quivered hard. He buried his head in Denise's shoulder, wrapping his arms around her.

"Shh. It's all right," she soothed. "Everything is all right. You're a sweet little boy. I'm glad you want to help people. That's good. But you understand that you need to do it with Dad or me, never ever by yourself."

"Yes." His voice was muffled, still buried in her shirt.

Phil squatted down so Andrew wouldn't have to look up at him.

"Look, Andy-bug," he said, turning him around to face him. "I'm so proud of you. I love that you would think about other people and go out and try to help them like that. I promise you that next year I will let you help me be Santa Claus. Maybe we'll make you a real elf costume or something."

Andrew rubbed his nose with the back of his arm. His face was smeared with tears. Phil sat down on the couch and pulled Andrew down beside him with Denise on Andrew's other side.

They sat in silence for a minute, Denise still rubbing her hands along Andrew's arms. "You're so cold." She pulled a quilt from the basket beside the couch and wrapped it over the top of all three of them. "Is that better?"

Andrew sniffed, but he was smiling now.

"Yeah."

The evening was black through the front window, only lit up by the Christmas lights on the neighborhood houses. But they were warm inside, snuggled together under the blanket. After a minute Denise looked at her watch.

"I've got to get the soup ready," she said. "We're supposed to be at Grandma's in an hour." Then she looked at Phil. "Shouldn't you be getting ready? I thought your appointment was at six."

Phil hugged Andrew closer.

"I'm not going," he said. "I can't. We almost lost Andrew today. I need to be here with you."

There wasn't any danger, but he was responsible for Andrew

getting lost. Somehow he had failed as a father, and his boy could have been killed.

"I'm not leaving you tonight," he said.

"Where were you going?" Andrew asked, turning his face to look up at Phil.

Phil pulled in a heavy breath and let it out quick.

"To be Santa Claus," he said.

Andrew jammed his elbow into Phil's side as he sat up straight. "But you have to go!" he said. "You need to! Think of the children!"

"He's right," Denise said, her eyes creasing with suppressed laughter as she hugged Andrew's head. "I know how you feel," she whispered to Phil. "We had a scare today. Andrew made a scary decision today to leave like he did." She reached over and squeezed Phil's hand. "But I love that he was thinking about giving to others on Christmas Eve. Look at how his associations of Santa Claus have already grown above what Santa will bring to him. That's because you do what you do at Christmas."

Phil was silent, his arm tight around Andrew.

"There's another family tonight who is grieving their lost child, Phil. You need to go and give them whatever comfort you can," Denise said.

He'd forgotten. Jack Taylor. It came slamming back on him, like he'd walked too close to a swing and it caught him upside the head. Another child lost. That family must bear it because Jack was not coming back. He wasn't standing outside the grocery store, ready to come home and be warmed up inside a blanket.

Phil blew out his breath. "You're right. I have to go."

"Of course you do, Dad," Andrew said.

The house looked the same as every other year, the white icicle lights lining the eaves and the wreath on the door. All of these things had been put up early in the season. They didn't know that before Christmas was up, tragedy would strike hard and close. The hurt of it hung over the house like a black rain cloud. How in the world was he going to summon a "ho ho ho" for this place?

Well. Best be at it. The job wouldn't go away just by standing here, staring in at it.

He got out and closed the door of his truck. The sound was sharp in the cold. His boots crunched on the salt rocks on the front step. He took a deep breath, and his breath came out in a white cloud. He reached up to knock.

"Phil!"

He jumped. Hannah trotted over from the garage, her hands clutching at the shawl around her shoulders.

"I've been waiting for you," she said, "I was going to catch you before you came in and ... well ... " She shrugged and sighed, and then handed him a slip of paper and walked back inside. She didn't really look at him, not for more than half a second. It was like the sight of his red coat and big white beard, the bells, all of it, were actually too painful. These were the things of Christmas that were supposed to equate with childhood memories, with joy and peace on earth. There was too much sorrow here to bear the clash of contrasts. What was he doing here anyway?

The Taylors had always been one of his favorite families, and Jack, well, Jack had been his own special buddy. Clear from the days when he was terrified of Santa Claus.

Every two-year-old is afraid of Santa Claus. That's how it had been with Jack. Only thing was, he never grew out of it. Travis, Jack's dad, was mortified that his kid was such a coward. Year after year he kept trying to force him into facing his fear.

"Go on, Jack," Travis would say, shoving him at Santa Claus. "Quit being such a big baby."

"I just don't want to, Dad. I just don't want to. Santa's for little kids."

Jack hung back, but Phil would watch him. He saw the way Jack's eyes followed the other kids as they told Santa their Christmas wish and got a present in return. Jack shrunk back into the corner and shrugged anybody off who tried to coax him out of there.

The year Jack was seven, Phil had called him over after all the other kids were done.

"Yeah, Jack. Get up on his lap," Travis said. He wasn't helping. Jack had started to come, but when his dad started up on him, he backed away again.

"I just don't want to. Santa Claus is dumb anyway."

"Jack, you're not leaving here until you do it," Travis said.

Jack took off running, but his grandpa had caught him around the middle and hugged him, patting his back while Jack hid his face.

"It's all right, Jack," Debbie said. "He's not going to hurt you. Go on and get up on his lap."

"I can't believe it!" Travis said. "He's seven years old, and he's still scared of Santa Claus!"

Phil held up a hand. "Dad, Mom, you just leave this alone. This is between me and Jack."

Travis humphed and folded his arms.

"Jack," Phil said again. "Jack."

At last the kid turned around, but his eyes stopped on Phil's beard and stayed there like that was as close as he could come to facing him.

"Come here, Jack."

Jack shook his head.

"I'm not going to grab you or anything. I just want to talk to you. You can bring Grandpa if you want, and you can stand as far away from me as you're comfortable. Do you think you can just come over here and talk to me?"

Jack hesitated and scuffled his feet along the carpet. His face was a mix of a scowl and a pout. Phil held up a hand at Travis, who took a step toward him. Jack glanced at his dad and took three steps toward Santa Claus. His eyes flicked again to Phil's beard and then away again.

"Now listen to me." Phil made his voice soft and gentle so that Jack had to lean in closer. "Listen to me. I want you to hear this. I know I look different, kind of weird, even a little scary, but I promise you I'm really a nice guy, and I would never do anything to hurt you. Do you believe that?"

Jack swallowed, actually glanced at Phil's face, and then

dipped his head in a nod. He had taken a step closer. Phil could almost feel the warmth of his little kid body.

"I want you to know that I love you," Phil said, and he looked him straight in the face. "I love all little children. Even the mean ones. And I want you to know I want to be your friend. I want you to be my special friend. What do you think about that?"

Jack's mouth quirked into a half smile, and he rolled his eyes, but he was close enough now that Phil slipped an arm around him.

"I don't want you to ever be afraid of Santa Claus. Ever," Phil said. "I want you to remember that I'm your friend. I only come around once a year, but I want you to know that you're going to be my special friend, and I love you, and I'll never do anything to hurt you. Will you remember that?"

Jack was full out smiling now, and he gave another nod.

"Okay, buddy. Now, give me a handshake, and that means that you and me will be friends forever."

Phil held out his hand, and Jack didn't even pause—just grabbed it and shook.

The next year he came in with his jolly "ho ho ho" and sat down on his chair. Jack was there, hovering behind the others, watching him. Waiting.

"Wait a minute, wait a minute," Phil said. "I got to have my buddy . . . Where's my friend? Where's Jack?"

The kid's face just blossomed into smiles. He walked right up to Santa Claus this time, brave as you please.

"Come here, buddy." Jack came right into his hug this time. "You remember our special secret?" he whispered.

Jack nodded his head and stuck out his hand. Phil shook.

"Now, Jack, do you want to be my special helper tonight? You can pull all the presents out of the bag. When you come to yours, just put it off to the side, and we'll have you come up last. Okay? Will that be all right?"

Jack had done it like that every year, first the handshake, and then Jack would help him hand out the presents.

"Santa Claus?" he asked. "Why do you wear your watch like that?"

Phil turned his wrist palm up and glanced at the face of his watch.

"Well," he said. "Back, eons ago, when I was a little guy like you, there was a man that was like a father to me, and he died. He always wore his watch with the face on the inside of his wrist, and so it's kind of my special way to remember him that I wear my watch like he did."

Jack grinned. "Cool," he said.

That man was actually his brother-in-law, but since Phil wasn't sure if Saint Nicolas actually ever had any in-laws, he left the story a little vague.

It was the first thing Phil noticed the next year, that Jack had got himself a watch and wore it with the face on the inside. Phil never mentioned it, but every year it was still there. It was another one of their little secrets.

Phil took a deep breath, let it out, and shook his head. He had to get out of this slump. How was he going to do this party when he was fighting to keep from breaking down himself?

He lifted his hand to knock when he saw the slip of paper Hannah had given him. He opened it. The handwriting was neat cursive, but neat or not, he was glad he had on his magic glasses.

> *The kids are confused, especially the older kids because they don't know if they should be happy in this sad time. Could you please explain it to them?*

Phil tucked it into his pocket.

"Hmph," he said. "Maybe someone should explain it to me first."

He did okay, really, handing out the presents. He held each of the little ones a bit tighter and gave them each a tiny bit more of his time and attention. He watched their faces until the smile reached their eyes.

But all the while Jack's mom, Debbie, sat in the rocking chair toward the back. She had her hands over her face, and her shoulders shook with her sobs. The adults huddled in clumps, talking together in low voices.

He shuffled in his bag that was obviously empty. Then he looked up at them.

"Well, that's pretty much it," he said. "But wait a minute, wait a minute. Somebody's missing. Where's my buddy?"

The adults in the back stopped talking, even the little ones in the front quieted. Little Ashley put her hand to her mouth and stared up at him, eyes wide.

"Where is he?" Phil asked.

Katie leaned into her mom. "Mom, doesn't he know . . . ?" she asked in a loud whisper.

Everybody was looking around and then looking at him.

Phil leaned toward the young ones in the front.

"You know what? I think he's here." He looked at the teenagers, at Alex, Jack's cousin, who had red puffy eyes. "I know he's here because he loved these family parties. He especially loved your Christmas party." Phil's voice caught, and he swallowed hard. "You know he would want you to be happy. It's Christmas, for heaven's sake! He doesn't want you to be sad. He wants you to be happy because it's Christmas, and Christmas should be a happy time of the year."

They were just looking at him, and somebody toward the back kept sniffing.

Phil turned, looked around at all of them, making a short gesture to Hannah, who brought out a rectangular package.

"It's hard not to be sad, I know. It's hard when we're not allowed to see him. That's one of the things that is really, really difficult about these kinds of separations."

Phil took a deep breath, and he looked directly at Debbie. Her arms were wrapped around herself, and one hand covered the lower half of her face. Her eyes showed above her hand, and there was so much sadness in them that Phil almost had to look away.

"But they're going to celebrate Christmas tomorrow where he's at too." He remembered the little girl that had died earlier this season. He could almost see them together in heaven. His voice caught. "It's going to be a very special Christmas for him, the first one of its kind." He was looking right at Debbie now as he talked. Debbie's hand had come down, and she was still. Her shoulders weren't trembling, and her arms relaxed like she was no longer trying to hold herself in. Travis squeezed a hand on her shoulder.

Phil kept talking, soothing. "Christmas is all about gifts. It started with the greatest gift of all, the gift of God's holy Son." Phil told them, and he handed the wrapped package to Debbie.

The paper crackled as she opened the package. It was a framed print by Greg Olsen, a picture of the Savior with a small boy looking up into his face.

"This gift isn't from Santa Claus," he told Debbie. "This doesn't have anything to do with me. It is a reminder from your family—to remind you where Jack is right now."

A sob came bursting out of her. Tears streamed down her face now, and a kind of peace settled across the pain in her eyes.

Phil stepped quietly until he was right up beside her.

"Look at him," Phil said. "Doesn't he look happy?"

Debbie's finger traced the little boy's face that was smiling up into the face of Jesus. She nodded.

"No," Phil said quietly. "I meant him." And he touched the face of the Savior.

"This gift is a two-way reminder," Phil said quietly. "One from your family to remind you where Jack is at, and the other part is from Jesus Christ, who has also given you some pretty great gifts. Not the least of these is that Jack will be returned to you one day, perfect and happy. And until that time, he will give you the gift of comfort and peace. Every Christmas from now on will be a reminder of Jack's death. But let it also be a reminder of the great gifts the Savior has given us, and let him come in and fill your life with the joy he intends for you to feel."

Debbie was rocking quietly now, her face upturned and her eyes looking far away from the rest of them. Phil touched her shoulder lightly, then squeezed Travis's hand, and quietly, so quietly, left the house.

The stars glittered overhead, and Phil stared up into the expanse of that Christmas Eve sky.

"Father in Heaven," he prayed, "give this family peace and comfort, and let them be filled with joy."

The tiniest wind ruffled his beard, stinging his eyes, and making the tears pool and spill over.

"Phil!"

He jumped.

Hannah was running up to him again, wiping at her eyes. She ran right up and wrapped him up in a hard hug.

"Thank you, thank you, thank you. You . . . you've made this party something that we'll always remember. Before you came some of my boys were saying 'I hope Santa Claus hurries up and gets here. I hate this party—it's not a party. It's nothing but a cry fest.' They said, 'If Santa Claus wasn't coming I'd go home, but my kids have to see Santa Claus.'"

Hannah leaned toward him. "Listen to them now," she said.

From a side door that was cracked open came happy voices, sounds of a family laughing together. He smiled. It was the sound of love.

"Alex started it," Hannah said. "He says, 'Remember the time that Jack brought that old chicken home?' And everybody started laughing! Imagine! And off it goes. They're still in there now. Everybody has a memory to share."

Phil gave her a smile. "Then you get on in there, and share it too," he told her. And to make sure she would, he walked to his truck and climbed in.

He lifted a hand in a wave, but she didn't see it. She had already gone back into that rectangle of light where her family was gathered.

The steering wheel was cold under his hands. He leaned forward and rested his forehead on it.

"Father." He paused, letting the peace of the moment swallow up the hurt in his heart. "Thank you," he said. "Thank you." He turned the key and drove away, leaving the Taylors to their Christmas. And it would be filled with joy after all.

Phil reached Mom's house at quarter after eight. The house glowed with lights, twinkling the joy of the season. From inside wafted the voices of the family. He could hear Lynn's loud guffaw over the top of everyone else. The little squeaking voices of Phil's grandkids were like music. He grinned. They sounded so young from out here. His smile was immediate and went clear through him. Bless them all.

Phil's boots crunched on the snow as he made his way to the back door. The screen squeaked as he pulled it open. Now the family was singing, all of them gathered together around the Christmas tree.

"Away in a manger, no crib for his bed."

Phil took up the song as he slipped through the door.

"The little Lord Jesus lay down his sweet head."

Tiptoeing down the hall, he passed into the spare room without anyone turning around from the circle around the Christmas tree.

"The stars in the heavens look down where he lay . . ."

Phil dressed quickly. He'd come prepared, hoping he'd be back in time. Then he laid the hat down and carefully spread the wig and beard on top of it, smoothing the curls with his fingers. It was the last time he would take it off this year. This year, like always, had made him a little more Christlike because he wore the suit.

Frank Jensen had brushed shoe polish into his beard every year to whiten it, and every year he needed a little less as his own natural beard took on the look of Santa Claus all by itself. Phil never could grow a good beard. But this one would do. Instead of shoe polish, he was changing inside, year by year. His heart was coming to be more like the heart of Santa Claus all the time.

"Silent night, holy night," came the sound from the living room. It was just the way it should sound, made with the mixed voices of his family. He closed the door quietly behind him, making sure it was locked, and then tiptoed down the hall. When he reached the living room, he let his voice out loud and strong to join the song.

"All is calm, all is bright," they sang, and he was gathered into the circle of them.

When they reached their own home, Andrew hurried to plug in the Christmas tree lights. The smell of wassail and sugar cookies gathered him in.

"Ah. There it is." Phil grinned at Denise. "You've been baking for Santa Claus." He couldn't wait.

"All right then, Andrew," Denise said, putting down the gifts they'd received from the rest of the family. "Now it's off to bed. You know what Santa Claus says about looking through his magic glasses and passing over the kids who aren't sleeping."

"Now, who told him that do you think?" Phil asked, shrugging out of his coat.

Andrew scampered off, whooping, and Phil caught Denise's arm.

"Come here," he whispered, and pulled her by the arm into the kitchen. He went into the laundry room and took the Santa Claus figurine down from the shelf. The paint had lost its stickiness; even the straw around the base of the manger was dry. He cradled it against his middle, and suddenly shy, brought it out. Denise was already laying the cookies onto a Christmas plate when he came out.

"Oh, Phil!" she said. "It's beautiful!"

Phil covered his mouth with a hand, but his smile was spilling out the sides. Denise was right. It had turned out good. Dry, the colors had both muted and sharpened. Even the white on the fur cuffs and trim that had given him so much grief had dried into soft shadows that made it look more real than anything he could have planned.

"It's amazing," Denise said. "May I?"

He handed it to her. She turned it this way and that, studying it. Finally she handed it back.

"Sometimes—I've seen this over and over again—when somebody feels strongly about what they're working on, they put something of that in it. I don't know quite how it happens, and it's not something you can recreate or even explain. But can you see it? Phil, this says everything you feel. It's like . . . your testimony."

Tears pricked at his eyes, and he wiped them with the back of his hand, embarrassed.

"That's exactly right," he said, and traced a finger over the face of Baby Jesus. "I was thinking . . . if you think he'll like it . . . I was going to give it to Andrew." He slipped it out like a confession and rubbed a hand up over his cheek.

"Oh Phil! That's perfect. That's really, really sweet. I think that's the sweetest thing I've heard all season."

He caught her arm and pulled her into a hug, resting his chin on her head.

"I love you too, Santa Claus," Denise said with a sideways smile.

"Do you think he's asleep yet?"

"Do pigs fly? It's Christmas Eve, Phil. That kid's got enough excitement to fuel him at least half the night."

"I saw Mommy kissing Santa Claus," he hummed, and kissed her. She pulled back, laughing.

Phil tweaked her nose and then pulled a hand towel off the rack, draped it over the figurine, and tiptoed down the hall to Andrew's room.

11

"Hey, Bug. He sat down on the floor beside Andrew's head. "Did you have fun tonight at Grandma's party?"

"Yeah." He was wriggling all over like a puppy wagging its tail.

"Dad, do you think when I grow up I can be Santa Claus too?"

"Well, I think so. If you want to. You know, every parent has a little bit of Santa Claus in them. Because they love their kids so much."

"I love you too, Dad."

"And you mean it that I'll be able to help you next year?"

"You bet. But not every time. That's too much for one little boy."

"Okay." Andrew grinned and snuggled down under his blankets.

"Good night."

Phil went slowly to the door, wondering how long it would take before he asked. His hand was on the doorknob before Andrew's voice came again.

"Hey, Dad. What's under the towel?"

Phil turned around, smiling.

"Well, son, it's just a little something. I made it, and I wanted you to have it. Because of the special secret that we have together, you know, about us being Santa's helpers."

Phil knelt down beside him.

"It's nothing really. Just a token. Something to help you understand why I do what I do."

He placed the figurine into Andrew's outstretched hands, and Andrew pulled the towel off. He studied it and touched the fur trim along the edge of the ceramic Santa's coat. His finger edged along the manger, and he traced the bundle of swaddling clothes inside. He turned it around, angled it this way and that, and then his mouth spread into a smile.

"That's the most important thing," Phil said. "Never, never forget that, Andrew. Always remember Jesus Christ at Christmas time."

"Cool," he said, grinning at Phil. "Thanks."

He was a good kid. He scuffled his hand through Andrew's hair.

"I love you, Andy-bug." Phil's voice almost caught. "Now you go on and go to sleep."

"Okay."

Once Andrew was settled, or at least quiet in his room, Phil pulled out a chair from the table and sat down.

"Well, he's down, but it'll probably be a few more hours before he's actually asleep."

"Thanks for making it back for the singing and the presents," Denise said. "How'd it go tonight?"

"Good, I think." He let the breath blow out. "Mmm. Can I have one of those?" He reached for a Christmas tree shaped cookie.

"They're for Santa Claus."

"That's what I hoped you'd say." He took a big bite, grinning. He washed it down with a cup of milk and then scratched a hand across his belly.

"Man, I'm tired."

"You never told me about the Kmart boy and his bed," Denise said, scooping the cookies onto a plate."

"It has a happy ending," he said, and told her briefly what

Judith had done earlier in the day. "Did I ever tell you about that other little boy that came into Kmart that same day as Cody? The one dressed all up in San Francisco '49ers duds?"

"Wasn't he the one who asked for the moon and all the amenities?" Denise asked.

"That's him. Alan Broderick Grady was his name. I'll bet his mom got him all that stuff just like she said she would. It's funny, Denise, how I can see it just clear as day in my mind. I can see Alan Broderick Grady tomorrow morning with boxes and wrapping paper to the ceiling where he's opened everything he can possibly wish for. His hands are on his hips and that sullen little face of his is just mad.

"He'll say, 'Is that all? That's not a very good Christmas.' There won't be a smile on anybody's face.

"And then I can see little Cody. He'll be sitting quietly, ever so quietly on his new bed, just watching the sky for it to get dark again so that he can go to sleep in his brand new bed. And his smile goes all the way to his heart."

"I can see it too," Denise said.

It was a couple hours later, when Phil and Denise were finally finished with the day and ready to head to bed themselves, when he flipped the light off in the hall as he passed Andrew's room. Then he flipped it back on and peeked through the crack in his door.

Andrew was buried to his face in the blankets again, all except one arm, and that was wrapped around the Santa Claus figurine that was pulled close on his bed, right up next to his face.

Man, he loved that kid.

"Merry Christmas, Andy-bug." He whispered it so soft that he couldn't even hear the sound of it himself. Then he blew him a kiss and went up for a well-deserved sleep. It was what every good Santa Claus deserved when it was Christmas Eve, and everything on his list was finally finished and done.

Discussion Questions

1. The title of this book is *Santa's Secret.* What was Santa's secret? How did it play a role in the book?

2. What was the most important thing to Phil? How did you come to that conclusion through the story?

3. How did Phil "become" Santa Claus? What was it that brought him to the realization that he had been missing something?

4. What did Phil like best about being Santa Claus?

5. How did Denise feel about Phil being Santa Claus?

6. Was Phil right in how he "told" Andrew about Santa Claus, or should he have said more?

7. How did Phil talk to Andrew about Santa Claus? What are the pros and cons in the way he did it?

8. Do you feel Phil carried the "Santa Claus" thing a little too far? Why or why not?

9. What is the significance of Santa Claus regarding Christmas? How important is he? How important should he be?

10. Phil felt strongly about giving every child as many "years of believing" as he could. Was this a good goal?

11. What kinds of things did Phil do to bring others toward Christ by being Santa Claus?

12. Was Phil's family better off or worse for his "Santa Claus-ing"?

13. Does the "magic" of Santa Claus really exist? Have you experienced it?

14. How is the magic of Santa Claus different from the magic of Christmas? Did Phil see a difference?

About the Author

Christy Hardman lives in Mapleton, Utah, with her family. She spends her time doing mom things with her five kids, putting out the local award-winning newspaper, the *Spanish Fork News*, and running with her wee dog. Christy runs half marathons annually, but one day plans to expand into triathlons and full marathons.

Christy has enjoyed writing articles for various publications for several years. She also enjoys making up quilt patterns that sometimes look good and sometimes don't. Long-term goals include finishing her degree (it's a long process with five kids) and keeping her house cleaner.

About Phil Porter

Phil was born and raised in Salem, Utah. He is married to Denise DeGraw; they are the proud parents of five children and grandparents of seven grandchildren. He's held various jobs that include radio announcer, police officer, custodian, restaurant manager, and bus driver. Phil has also enjoyed serving in Church callings and has been a part of Lion's Club International for over twenty-five years. He enjoys fishing, cooking, traveling, and being Santa Claus every Christmas.